Academy Arts Press 2019 Short Story Anthology

ISBN 978-1-7347313-1-6

Cover Design by Mandy Morreale

academyartspress.com

TABLE OF CONTENTS

The Biscuit Board / *Mary Popham* 1

Great Friends / *Marc Hockl* 10

Doc / *David Gaylor* 15

The Rest Of The World / *Gary Wadley* 20

Blithe / *Margie Marek* 30

Strange Impressions / *Victor Salia* 33

Beyond The Sea / *Ross Touhy* 47

Would I? Could I? Should I? / *Mandy Morreale* 53

Gills / *Gary Wadley* 62

Flight Of The Eye / *Sheri Hawthorne Carbone* 82

The House With Two Front Doors / *Lucy Mills* 92

Newspaper Man / *Malarie Drake* 108

Ulricke Klackenbach / *Michael Noonan* 116

Ancestors not Calm / *Vin Morreale, Jr.* 135

The Biscuit Board

Mary Popham

My girlfriend Gracie Adamo and I hauled a load of metal folding chairs to Mobile. Then across town, we made a pick-up from Econo Printing, one of my regular customers. I drive a semi-truck and have a freight broker's license to act as my own agent, so I book a load for the return trip up I-65 … no empty trailer on the flip flop. Yeah, I'm a big guy getting a bald head and a beer belly. But my worn shirt and worker boots might fool a person. I know my trade and how to run a business, how to save expenses, how to make a profit. But I don't take chances, and I ain't killing myself over a job. I deliver mostly dry freight; it saves a lot of stress because you get a perishable load and it means a strict deadline. Besides that, liability insurance for refrigerated transport eats into my profit big time.

Heading north from Mobile, Gracie and I were somewhere past halfway home to Louisville with boxes of posters, stock photos and twelve hundred copies of a book called *The Biscuit Board.* Now usually I don't sign on for a rush job, but this particular book was making big sales throughout the country and Wal-Mart stores needed them in Louisville—now.

My buddy at the Econo terminal gave Gracie a copy of the book and she flipped through it. "My gosh," she said. "I thought this was some kind of cookbook but guess what."

"What?" I said, keeping my eyes on that long ribbon of asphalt disappearing 'neath our wheels.

"This book is about a high level group of businessmen; investors, contractors and you know, kingpins." She turned on the overhead and read to herself for a few minutes. "Something about them setting up operations all across the South, taking over the markets, and influencing Wall Street."

I smiled at her look of concentration, loving the way her brow knits when she holds a book close to her eyes. Even after being all day on the road, I could still smell the Ivory Soap that Gracie uses. Takes me back to a peaceful kind of feeling.

"It says here that this bunch has infiltrated the panel that set up regulations and therefore bypassed the safeguards." She turned and stuck the book behind the curtain that separates the cab from the sleeper. "I'm gonna have to read some more on that," she said.

I smiled to myself, again appreciating having Gracie with me on this overnight. I had traveled alone since my uncle retired and gave me a good deal on his truck, but even though we're together all the time I still hate to leave her for even one night.

Behind the cab is a single bunk sleeper wide enough for both Gracie and me to be comfortable. I steam-cleaned the carpet just for her.

It was nighttime and Gracie played her favorite CD; The Andrews Sisters, with tunes like *Don't Sit Under the Apple Tree* and *Rum and Coca Cola.* I said, "Honey, those songs came out in World War II. Don't you like anything from this century?"

But she just grinned at me, showing those cute dimples and little white teeth and shook her shoulders like she's doing the boogie-woogie sitting there in the truck cab. If I was driving by myself, I'd probably be listening to somebody from 2013 like Kenny Chesney. But come to think of it, I like older music. Classics, like the Allman

Brothers and Waylon and Willie. and I know a lot of thirty-year-olds like them, too. Gracie, she likes all kinds of music, and told me her all-time favorite song is *Across the Universe* by the Beatles.

Gracie and I have got this shorthand that Mom told me usually develops between old married couples. It started fairly early with my nickname. My last name being Woodford, it didn't take much imagination to shorten it to Woody. Starting in first grade, I heard jokes like "Knock Knock. Who's there? Woody. Woody who? Woody ya want!" Then it moved up, if you can believe it, to "How much wood would a woodchuck chuck…" My Mom and Dad claimed they didn't do it on purpose when they named me Charles. Charles? Chuck?

But when Gracie says "Chuck," it's different. She purses her sweet lips out where I can see her little white teeth and imagine her tongue just behind them. When she says "Woody," it's usually shorthand for "Would ya like to . . . " and in my mind I fill in the blank and say, "Yes, I would."

Little Gracie and I clicked that first night I picked her up in the Napa River Grill. Only she taps me on the arm if I say "picked up" to anybody outside our house. But she *is* a waitress there and I *did* give her a ride home.

The Napa Grill is pretty upscale, but hey, I stopped by one night when I was dressed up. Its slogan should have told me I was paying for atmosphere. "A taste of northern California in Louisville's own backyard." Which means they got a nice wine list and steak tender as a mother's love, but their portions aren't like an all-you-can-eat buffet. But then, if I hadn't of gone in, I wouldn't have met Gracie.

Since she works the day shift now, I hang out for happy hour, and then we leave and eat at home.

We'd just pulled out of the rest area past Sonora and hadn't yet picked up any speed when I noticed two heavy duty trucks boxing me in. When I signaled to pass the smaller one in front of me, the Dodge Ram in back of us pulled alongside my cab in the left lane. When I slowed down thinking maybe he would go around, the lone driver ahead of me slowed too and closed up the space. They had me cornered. I didn't want to panic Gracie, but she saw what was happening, anyway.

"What are these fools doing?!" she yelled.

I forced a calmness I didn't feel. "Honey, watch out now, I'm going to put the hammer down. He's gonna move or I'm gonna bite me somebody's bumper!"

I kicked myself for not paying attention to a gut feeling I had gotten at the last rest stop when I noticed the three people in the Dodge Ram parked beside us. Here I had the love of my life sitting in the cab with me and more precious than any cargo I've transported since I bought my uncle's truck three years ago. Why wasn't I more careful when I spotted that custom-built monster vehicle pull into the next space? I thought there was something odd about the truck with the bench seat holding three people who just sat there with their heads turned away. I always leave my engine running, but I thought sure I had locked the cab when Gracie and I went to the restrooms.

One thing I like about my job is the people I meet, and even if I don't talk to them, I kinda get a look at their lives by what I overhear them saying, or what I see them wearing, or maybe their license plates; just little things that maybe some travelers would miss. But there was something suspicious about those three: a tall, heavy-set woman dressed in a denim jacket and jeans, one white man with a cowboy hat, and one black man with a turtleneck sweater. Not that they shouldn't have all been together, but they acted odd. Why did they stay in the truck? Why did all three have their heads turned? And now to find them trying to force me off the road brought all my forecasting back, and I slammed my palm against the steering wheel so hard it hurt. I should have known better!

I had all kinds of things rushing in my head when I stepped on the gas and touched the bumper of the smaller truck in front of me. The truck bucked a little ahead but dropped its speed more and more as if the driver dared me to hit him again.

Out my side window, the Dodge Ram was pulled up to run even with me. Somebody leaned out the passenger window and yelled, "Pull over or I'll shoot!" I couldn't see a gun but as we passed under a highway light pole, I caught a glimpse of a big-shouldered man in a ski mask.

"Call 911!" I yelled to Gracie as I gripped the steering wheel, fighting between slowing down so as not to hit the truck in front of me, or speeding up to ram it again. Everything I know said don't pull over, but it wasn't my life or this stupid load of books and paper I was thinking about. I just pictured my Gracie either going through my windshield or getting shot by a trained killer.

"Our cell phones! They're gone!" yelled Gracie searching her pockets, the console between us, and the charging outlet where I had put my cell.

Time stopped and I worried what was going to happen, trying to figure the best thing to do. I've been crazy over Gracie since the first moment I laid eyes upon her. I had to protect her, above all else.

I guess we'd both had enough with being lonesome and decided to play out this thing we've got going, at least, until one or the other or maybe even both of us decide it's over. I can't imagine that, for we moved in together within a week's time. I know it was awful quick to be taking a step like that and we didn't even know whether I liked her cooking or if she could stand my socks and shorts strewn out from the bedroom to the bathroom and back. But as it happens, I love her homemade meatballs with her family's secret Italian sauce. And about my underwear…well, she's got me to where I pick it up and throw it in the hamper. It's a learning process, is what Gracie says.

"Be cool," said Gracie to me as she put a soft hand on my arm. "Be calm. Don't make any sudden moves or try to jump them or anything."

In a rip-roaring rage, I could barely hear Gracie's voice. I gasped in deep breaths of air and rubbed the back of my neck hard, my anger splitting my head open. If I could slam that truck ahead of me, leave them a tangled pile of smoldering metal, I would. I was praying that the Dodge Ram would get in front of me, too, so I could crush them both into flaming pieces. But Gracie was here with me.

I had barely pulled my truck onto the shoulder and came to a stop with the engine still running, when my little Gracie jumped out, all five-foot-two of her and stood away from the cab with her hands loose from the sides of her body like she wasn't holding a weapon.

"Take it easy. Take it easy," she said, to the young bearded man who jumped from the truck that had been driving ahead and was now pulled off the road in front of us. He wore a red bandanna wrapped around his head and tied in back.

"Leave the keys! Leave the keys!" the guy yelled at me. He walked up close to Gracie and I jumped out of the truck and ran to grab him. Suddenly, I felt my arms pinned back by the two men from the rest stop who had jumped out of the Dodge Ram behind us. The white man wore a ski mask and a cowboy hat which made him look like the Lone Ranger. The black man wore a turtleneck sweater.

I heard Gracie's voice. She was calm. "It's okay, Woody. It's okay."

The guy in the turtleneck slapped my pockets and down the sides of my legs and into my socks and the tops of my boots, while the one in the cowboy hat climbed behind the wheel of my truck.

I watched the young punk with the red bandana in front of Gracie. He reached around and barely touched her back pockets. "She ain't got no gun," he said, and his voice sounded like a kid's. I looked close at his face. The beard hid his cheeks and chin, but the lines creasing his forehead and around his eyes added too much age. I wondered if he'd already spent time in the pen and became even more of a hoodlum there.

The big woman in denim had scooted over under the wheel of the Dodge Ram. She flung her arm out the window pointing north, and then screeched onto the highway. The young bearded guy with the red bandana got back in his truck and hightailed it her. Neither one of the vehicles had a license plate, just some kind of paper in the back window that looked like it could be a Print-on-Demand temporary tag. Whatever it was, I couldn't read either one.

As I watched Cowboy studying my gear shift and touching my dash control unit, I wanted my little snub-nose in my hand so bad I could taste it. But I had left it in the bottom drawer on my side of the dresser. Because of Gracie. She almost had a fit when she found out I even owned a gun and I promised her I wouldn't carry it on this trip.

Damn! First time I really needed it and I'd left it at home!

I figured they weren't going to shoot us, but I had to stand there and watch the guy in the black turtleneck jump up in the passenger side, slapping the dash of my truck.

"Haul it on outta here!" he yelled at Cowboy.

That was my engine I heard being revved by a stranger, and I fought back wanting to run up to that door and pull him out on his ass and beat him 'til he couldn't walk. But I looked over at Gracie. Her eyes were all sorrowful, but she stood there calm and still. So I just turned back and watched my truck pick up speed and disappear down the highway.

There was a cold ache beginning deep in me, one of anger and revenge and a painful hurting, too. It was a raw deal to work hard and then watch helpless while two goons make off with something I worked so hard for, took care of, and now the next time I saw it, if I ever saw it again, who knew what kind of shape it'd be in?

I wrapped my arms around Gracie, and we stood there holding each other tight. It hit me how lucky we were, still alive, and not hurt. She started crying but I think it was because she was mad, not scared.

"Sonsa bitches!" she yelled out into the night, then again, louder. "Sonsa bitches! I hope the police catch you and you all rot in jail!"

And all the time, I'm patting her and saying, "It's all over, Gracie, Honey, and we're okay. It's all over."

No truck, no phones, but at least I still had my trucker wallet chained to my belt loop. The hijackers had moved fast. Cars and trucks were passing, but I guess, were too busy to see what was going on. The whole thing had flashed by like a bad dream.

I wondered if Gracie would ever go with me again on a run. Would she remember this nightmare and from now on, send me away with just a sandwich and a kiss?

Gracie finally turned to me and said, "We have just been hijacked to prevent an exposé."

It took a minute to realize she was talking about the book.

Gracie's eyes were gleaming, and she nodded her head up and down like she had just figured out a mystery.

"This Biscuit Board controls a lot of business in the South, and that's how it got its name. You know, the North likes cold bread and the South likes its bread hot?"

I thought more likely it was just brazen, no-good thieves looking to pawn a bestselling book on the black market. I went over in my mind what I had learned in the Armed Robbery Response training, rehearsing what I would tell the police when they stopped to investigate two people standing out here on the side of the highway, alone in the cool night breeze without a vehicle.

"Yessir," Gracie paced back and forth. "They don't want their whole operation broadcast to the world, so they think they'll be able to suppress it by stealing that truckload of books! But when this story gets out, it'll make people want to buy the book all the more!"

I felt my shoulders drop in relief, as I watched her face and saw that the trauma of our ordeal would never leave its mark.

Not on my Gracie.

Great Friends

Marc Hockl

We instantly woke to the sound of shouting. Squinting heavy eyes revealed 0315 on the small clock resting atop the two-foot-high wall of sandbags stacked inside our tent. The arctic heaters were blasting, which didn't make sleeping in an Air Force arctic sleeping bag any easier.

This was life in UNPROFOR, the United Nations Protective Forces stationed in Northern Croatia. We were part of a US Air Force Medical unit dropped in the middle of the brutal Serbian conflict, a war in everything but the name.

"Snow call," the Chief blared again, "Assemble outside." Chief's face bore a jovial smile, as if waking at 3 AM to do menial labor somehow kindled his dour spirit.

Rather than assemble, I motioned for a few of the guys to follow me. We went to a supply *connex*, a lockable freight container, and opened it. Inside were various medical supplies. Our objective was the dozens of NATO litters. We opened a few of them and carefully laid ten or twelve others on each open litter. A quick run through the heavy falling snow, already a half a foot deep, brought us to the hundred and ninety-eight troops shifting from foot to foot in a vain effort to keep warm. The 'Prime Beef' contingent, as we called them, also arrived at this time, armed with shovels usually relegated to sandbag filling, and while not designed for shoveling snow, they were all we had. Prime Beef were a squad of construction engineers, comprised of carpenters, electricians, mechanics, and other handyman specialties. If a makeshift tool was needed, these were the guys to call. And they had indeed brought forth about twelve foot-long 2x2s, each with a flat board screwed to one end.

Chief was already barking at the shifting, shivering troops.

"We got word a blizzard is coming, and this probably won't stop until about noon or so. We're looking to get about four feet of snow. I don't need to tell you we will be sleeping in it if that much snow collapses our tents. So get busy! The hospital tents are mostly under the hanger, so I want six of you to head over there and use the litters to cart as much stuff as practical. The rest of you, focus on keeping the tents from collapsing under the weight."

My buddy, Gunny, grumbled as he looked up at me in frustration. He wasn't exactly known for his patience..

"What else have we got to look forward to for the next six months?" I smiled, which pissed him off even more.

We worked in shifts in that bitter cold, which meant ten minute breaks every two hours. At that pace, we finished at 1 PM, just as the blizzard had started to taper off. I was heading off to the mess tent to get something warm when I ran into Gunny coming the other way.

"The ER has been quiet, but we popped out every few hours to brush off your Humvee ambulances," he told me, a misty puff of breath hanging in the cold air. "The Norwegians said nothing is coming in from their sectors yet. So I'm just humping it to get some chow."

"That's good," I nodded. Keeping the ambulances at the ready was a top priority. Quick access meant the difference between life and death, and those Humvees were just as suited for this type of climate as the deserts of the Middle East. "Anyone inside need to go for rehab or scans or anything downtown?"

"No," he grinned. "I know you're itching to take those Humvees out in the snow. I hear the roads are all closed in Zagreb but we both know that won't stop the Humvees. And it sure as hell won't stop you if we get the call for an extraction."

"Look, you know I'd be glad to have you on my ambulance crew, but we can't have all our best clumped into one work section. Chief's orders. Besides, I am down in the ER more often than not these days, on-duty or off." I watched his eyes narrow, then drift off to the frozen white horizon. Gunny was the kind that needed to feel useful 24/7, and this posting was everywhere he didn't want to be. I changed the subject to cheer him up.

"Hey, it was hilarious to run into Admiral Borda the other day. And you killed me when he asked where you were in Shield and Storm, 'Uh, Saudi,' you told him. It was classic. Truly classic."

I watched one corner of his mouth curl up, despite his mood. "Yeah. That was some time, wasn't it?" he mumbled, with the distant stare that crept into the eyes of those who had seen real action. "Some time," he repeated.

"I didn't know you were there for that, but I didn't get to run across many friendlies in all my secret squirrel work. Classified locations and all."

"That was a time," he said again. "Hey, you need me to go with you to teach front line aid to those foreign forward observers again?"

"Let's ask Chief. You got some language skills. I'm training a few Polish guys, and it would be good to have someone help me speak some Slovak, instead of playing Pictionary with the others who don't understand me."

"Don't give me that," Gunny laughed, as he punched my shoulder. "You speak that crap like a native."

I grinned. Gunny always could see right through me. "Well, I think I have the whole Eastern Bloc countries covered. The Russians understand me, and Sergei is usually at the ER anyways checking on his troops. I am heading to standby as the Czech minesweepers clear out another section around the tarmac."

The truth was, there were only three of us among nearly two hundred deemed fluent enough to qualify as interpreters. And when a multinational coalition goes to battle, we were the guys they depended on to make things go smoothly, or at least as smoothly as war can go.

Some weeks later found me dashing out to the tarmac with a Bell 212 chopper flying in several patients from Sector South. As I shouted to move out, a bone white hand grabbed my arm just above the glove. The icy fingers slid the end of my Gortex jacket and thermal sleeve up, exposing my bare arm. The air that day wasn't cold, but the hand sure was. It belonged to a Norwegian Medic who had the haunted eyes of someone who had seen far too many horrors, way too much death. As he gripped my arm, he nodded to the bloody form laid out on the stretcher. It took me a moment to recognize the familiar face contorted with pain. His name was Sergei, one of the Polish peacekeepers I had taught only weeks before. This day, he needed no interpreter to communicate his final moment of agony.

The pale Norwegian pointed to the small bag on the litter beside Sergei's body.

"Hes brains are in dat bag dare," he whispered.

Such was the real language of war.

Sergei was but the first of many good friends I would make over there, only to reunite with them in the ER. Some alive. So many dead.

Andrei, a Brazilian soldier, came in with his right leg covered in tar and his left foot held on by only a small patch of skin. It was as if his foot was blown off, but the tongue of his boot resisted enough to prevent his foot from totally separating. As I tried to calm his anguish, I discovered that what I assumed was tar turned out to be nothing but charred flesh, burnt down to the bone. I had no words for the terror he must have been feeling at that moment. We both knew we would have to amputate the charred right leg just above the knee, and there would also be no way to save his left foot either.

I was able to spend more time with Andrei, only because there was a rehab clinic named Rebro located in downtown Zagreb, which fitted and acquainted prosthetics for patients. But seeing friends come back in pieces is something you cannot easily forget.

It was not my last time in a combat theatre. The nations would change; Croatia to Afghanistan to Iraq, but the uniforms all look the same when stained with blood.

These days, I lay awake at night, afraid to sleep. Somehow wishing and fearing another 3 AM snow call. Was it foreshadowing my time there? Or my time in the military as a whole?

A total of fifty-one inches of snow fell that night in Croatia, the worst snowfall that country had suffered since September 1941.

But for me, it was only the first of fifty-one hells to follow.

Doc

David Gaylor

He was tired… Just plain wore out.

After prescribing a medicinal cough syrup earlier in the day to little Billy Martin, and praying it wasn't the whopping cough, then heading five miles out of town to deliver Millie Thompson's baby boy, almost losing her in the process…he now had been summoned by a young lad to return to town to his medical office (and "as needed" undertaker establishment) on Hell Street, to dig a lead ball out of drunken muleskinner's belly, due to the former running his mouth way too much during a card game at the Colorado Saloon. No telling whether the stranger would need both of his "before and after" skills before the day was through.

Some folks never learn, do they?

As his buggy slid through the crust of snow that had fallen earlier the previous night, and his calloused fingers tightened on the reins, a thought came to him, *How long has it been since he started up his practice?*

Let's see... apprenticed with Old Doc Moore, in Hays, Kansas in '31 for a few years. Soaked in as much knowledge as he could, he then moved to the godforsaken town of Canyon Diablo, known to all as Devil's Canyon, thirty-five years ago before this very day. All the while, starting life, extending life, and tending to those entering the afterlife.

These old hands had washed off a lot of blood, set broken bones, spanked life into newborn babies and placed many a penny on the eyes of dead men, with no apparent end in sight.

Letting out a sigh, which created a misty cloud that would soon crystalize on his gritty beard and wire-rimmed spectacles, he spurred Old Rusty eastward on towards town, silently hoping he would beat nightfall and still have enough time to divert the Grim Reaper's attention from the muleskinner.

As the wind started to pick up, the aging doctor realized he had not packed for the cold. He thought he'd have been back to town hours ago, but Millie Thompson's hemorrhaging had taken longer to stop than he figured, and for her and her newborn's sake, he had stayed until he was sure he could leave her in somewhat of a more stable condition with her farmer-husband Jedidiah there to look after them. He planned on checking back in on her and the baby in a week or so. God willing.

But now, with no food or water and just a thin buggy blanket covering his lower body, the pressing matter ahead was turning to his own well-being, for a strange chill was beginning to enter his body, even as Old Rusty, his ever faithful four-legged companion, trotted briskly away from the daylight sun that had started its own descent beyond the Cider Mountain ridge behind them in the western skies.

A storm was brewing, and it was surely no place for a man, let alone an old doc and his beast, to be out in all alone.

As the wind began to moan and ice pellets stung his exposed cheeks, a sudden sense of urgency overtook him. He pulled his coat closer to warm himself, but to no avail. His chill deepened and he knew as a doctor that cold can set in hard and fast with age, thinner blood and all. He beckoned Rusty to canter faster through the escaping daylight and quietly cursed himself for not bringing a lantern to light their way. The dropping night temperature and blowing wind that swirled viciously around them wasn't helping his predicament much neither.

As he snapped the reins, his left arm brushed his left side coat pocket, reminding him of the small bottle of his special tonic medicine he had placed there earlier in the day, which did much to quiet coughs, not to mention bringing a soothing warmth to one's body. Maybe it would help him rid him of this chill that was gradually taking hold of his extremities.

Just one sip. No more.

Steadying Rusty's reins with one hand, he uncorked the welcomed bottle and, tilting his head back, allowed the crimson-colored elixir to gently slide down his throat.

"Not much farther to travel, old boy," he said to Rusty. His raspy words hung mockingly in the chilly night air, punctuated by the echo of hooves on crusted snow. Maybe just a mile and a half or so ahead and he'd be back to his buck stove, hot chowder, and blessedly warm bed. Of course, that'd be after tending to that damn fool muleskinner, who'd probably have to pay him with beaver pelts for his services and inconvenience.

The wind's howl was picking up and he sensed the snow was deepening as they closed in on town, confirmed by a slight skid of his buggy wheels over a dip on the quickly disappearing path on which they trod. But the cold… this savage cold… would not loosen its grip. Maybe one more pull of his elixir might help. Not much longer to go, he surmised.

Squinting through the frozen droplets on his glasses, he could just make out a hint of town lights twinkling in the distance. Shouts of instinctive joy rose within him. Estimating he was yet a mile or so out, he took another quick taste, just as Rusty's front leg found a deep, vacated gopher hole buried under the freshly fallen snow.

It all happened in an instant; the snap of Rusty's leg and the horse's anguished scream, coupled with his own startled cry, echoed thinly against the howling wind.

Moments later, maybe longer, his senses started to return to him. He found himself looking upwards at the now blackened sky, the heavy wooden buggy lying sideways on top of him. He slowly, achingly, brushed a creeping layer of snow off his heaving chest and freezing face, then raising up on one trembling elbow, he saw how the buggy's front wheel hub was pinning his waist to the frozen ground. But oddly, he felt no pain from either the compound fracture in his right leg, nor the slowly reddening snow beneath him, which undoubtedly led back to a ghastly wound that he, even as a doctor, probably didn't want to see.

Looking to his right side, he could just make out Rusty in the pelting snow lying on his side, laboriously breathing and also unable to move. *There, there, old boy,* he thought. *That young lad that fetched us earlier will alert the town folk in time for them to find us. And I'll ask them good folks to help you out of your misery.*

I'll miss you, old friend, he whispered in a voice fragile as the snowflakes.

Miraculously, the elixir bottle was lying just within his reach, the only thing unbroken out on that empty path. Grasping it, he gingerly laid his old body back, only to realize that the wind and biting snow had stopped, leaving a clear canopy of stars overhead. With a gentle sip, he looked to find the North Star and the Big Dipper, just as he did when he was a mere boy many years before. The waves of subsiding cold and warmth were gradually replaced by a gentle peacefulness. As the stillness of the night allowed him to now rest his tired bones, his waning thoughts turned to the muleskinner. *I hope he can hold on 'til I can tend to him…one way or t'other.*

But for now, maybe he could just close his eyes…and rest a spell…but only for a little while.

The Rest of the World

Gary Wadley

Leo saw it when he went to make his morning coffee - a little fiddler crab in the kitchen sink, standing on the scratched porcelain, waving its one fat claw like a truce flag. He studied it for a moment, then filled the percolator with water and coffee and placed it on the gas stove, which let out a soft fart when he turned on the gas.

The crab was still there when the coffee began to percolate, though it had moved a few inches and seemed to be picking at a piece of scrap in the sink. Leo thought the crab might go back down the sink drainpipe that led under the house to the beach, then to the gulf and off to the rest of the world.

"The screen at the end of the drain has come off," he said, maybe even aloud.

Leo lived alone and often conversed with himself, with the animate and the inanimate, no longer caring to distinguish between the two. After the passing of his wife, he decided it made no difference. He would talk to a chair or a rock as readily as to a bird or a cat. Speaking to things comforted him as one is comforted by holding a smashed finger or rubbing a bumped head, so it was nothing that he should speak to the little crab.

"You should go home," he said, though he really didn't mind the visiting crab. Not long ago he would have gently picked up the creature, avoiding its one big claw, and carried it out of the house, back to the beach. But he was old now and tired and inclined to let things do as they pleased. He remembered how, when he was a boy, the fiddlers would swarm over the beach at low tide, colorful in the sun as they emerged from their little holes in the sand. He figured they must be eating and courting, the males impressing the females with their one big claw, but always in the end the tide would return, and they would retreat to their burrows to be covered by the water. It delighted him that a crab could live underwater and in the air at the same time.

When the coffee was ready, Leo sat at the scarred dining table and thought about his day. He knew weather was coming because his knees and shoulders ached. He did not mind weather so much now because he no longer went out on the water and was content to watch whatever blew in from the gulf through his front window. But he did not care for the light of the sun, because as it broke on the water it blinded one; and after a while the eyes got milky, and sometimes sores that would not heal bloomed on the arms and nose. When he thought of this, he felt sad for those who still had to go out on the water.

He heard scratching in the sink and remembered the fiddler. Perhaps he would make the effort to put him in a mug and free him on the beach at low tide.

Then came a knock on the door. Then another knock and someone called his name. He knew the voice. It was the woman from the government, come to bother him again. He knew if he did not answer she would try all the doors and eventually return and threaten to put him in a home, so he sighed and finally went to open the door.

The government woman was Miss Claudia Brown. Leo didn't actually know if she was a Miss, though he couldn't see how a woman like her could be anything else. Her thick body was topped by a broad and sad face, that itself was topped by a wild arrangement of grey hair. Her hair reminded Leo of seagulls fighting over a scrap of fish. Proud of her status as a government worker, she exuded a self-important and efficient uselessness.

Leo opened the door wide, then retreated quickly as Miss Brown charged inside. He was raised to be polite and said nothing.

"Leo," she said. He could not tell if it was a question or a statement and looked at her as though she were a strange chair that had turned up in his house. "Leo," she said again, "As you know, we're worried about you. That you're not getting enough to eat. That you're all alone. What if we…?"

"I eat government cheese," he said quickly. "Those big bricks last a long time." Leo had learned that the word *we* was seldom used for his benefit.

She shook her head, sent the seagulls flying. "Yes, but… What?" Miss Brown heard a faint scratching sound and turned toward the noise. "You have company?" She looked surprised. She was sure Leo never had company.

"Yes. I have a friend now," he nodded toward the kitchen. He wanted to tell her it was really none of her business but knew that would only encourage the government-sanctioned part of her, so he simply said, "I have a visitor in the kitchen sink."

There were times he envied those naughty boys who could emit gas at will.

Miss Brown looked at him, showing large teeth. "In the sink?" She asked this as though she might have discovered something, a way to untie a difficult knot.

Leo nodded and she walked into the kitchen uninvited, as a cat upon a bird. Slow. Focused.

"The sink?" she repeated. The little crab was still there and stopped scratching as soon as the government worker's huge face rose over the rim of the sink. The creature tilted his eye stalks back and stared at her, then began to wave its large claw.

"Hello," it said.

Of course, Claudia Brown reasoned she did not actually hear what she had heard. Crabs do not speak. The floor joint must have creaked, or Leo had made a sound in the other room. Crabs, even intelligent ones (if there were such a thing) had no voice box. No speaking apparatus at all. The only thing Claudia had ever seen come from a crab's mouth was bubbles and she'd eaten enough crab to know there was no tongue, no lips, no speech.

"How?" she asked, not the crab, but Leo, who had remained at the front door.

"How what?" he replied.

Miss Brown stood for a moment looking around the kitchen, then down to the little crab that was busy again with something in the sink. She cleared her throat, then spun and left the house, leaving a pleasantly empty space in her wake.

After a moment Leo entered the kitchen and asked, "What happened? What did you do?"

"Nothing. I just said, 'Hello'," said the crab.

Leo nodded, amazed at the power of simple words.

Claudia Brown sat with Vince Gooden in the Redundant Café, a small place in Gainesville where they would meet when privacy was required; where it was unlikely anyone from Cedar Key would see them. Claudia liked to imagine they met there because it was intimate. After all, Vince was *the* developer in Levy County, as well as her very special friend. Their arrangement had been financially and personally beneficial and she was excited about the news she was about to deliver. She blew on her coffee and said, "He's crazy and it won't be long before he's gone."

"How long?" Vince asked. He knew there were no relatives, no third party claims on the house. With Leo gone, he would purchase the waterfront house at auction, remodel, and sell it for a fortune.

"That depends," Claudia said. "He's definitely senile." She paused and smiled up at Vince, pleased at her own cleverness. "He keeps a fiddler crab as a pet in his sink. Even talks to it!" It was only a little lie. She did not mention it was the crab that talked. "I need to do a few more observations, document another episode of nuttiness, then we can petition for a hearing. He'll be found incompetent, made a ward of the state and shuttled off to a home."

Vince drew a cigarette from a pack and tapped it on the table as he looked at Claudia. *So homely*, he thought, *but useful; and beachfront property was . . .* He felt Claudia's leg brush against his under the table and he lit the cigarette, blowing a smoke cloud over her head.

Leo and the crab became friends, as much as one can become friends with a crab. The man was grateful the little creature had scared away the government woman and did not mind conversation. The crab (so he said) was grateful for the scraps of food the man left in the sink. Leo chose not to fix the screen over the drainage pipe.

After a few days, the man carefully placed the little creature on a plate at his table so that they could talk more comfortably. He gathered a bit of seaweed and a little sand from the beach and put it on the plate so that the crab would feel at home. Some evenings they talked for hours, the man leaning close so that his friend would not have to strain his tiny voice.

"You are hard on the outside and soft on the inside," Leo would say.

The crab would then tap the plate with his claw, as though making a toast and say, "And you are soft on the outside and hard on the inside."

Leo grinned. He was not surprised the crab knew this because crabs eat many things as they go about cleaning up the waters. He himself had gained a bit of knowledge from eating blue crabs and stone crabs when he could get them. He boiled them until they reddened like the evening sun and cracked them open to get at the succulent meat and juices. He did not mention this to the little crab, of course. All in all he was glad for the company, and though it occurred to him that he might be going crazy, surely there was no harm in talking to a fiddler crab. Still, the crab talked back, and this made him wonder about the nature of his madness. In any case, he was careful to bathe at least a twice a week and he brushed his teeth every night, so he reasoned he couldn't be too far gone.

One evening Leo read the crab an official looking letter he had just received, then set it down quickly, as though it might burst into flame at any moment.

"You have been very kind to me," said the crab. "Men don't like us much, probably because of our cousins, the spiders. Though on the whole, spiders are not so bad." Leo liked spiders and took pains to place them outside whenever he found them wandering around the house. Even the black widow, who could not help how she was born. "I think," the crab continued, "that I will help you. And that the next visit from the government lady should be at nine p.m. on the night of the fourteenth."

Leo was surprised that a crab should know of dates and times. He reasoned that wild things probably knew a great deal about such things -- time and season and tide and sun and moon -- for that is how they lived; but to place a time and number upon a day impressed him greatly and he knew he still had much to learn.

"Why the fourteenth?" he asked.

The crab shrugged, though of course this was impossible. "It will be a full moon and…" The little eye stalks looked up to the man and seemed to blink, waiting.

"It will be low tide," said the man.

"Precisely," said the crab. "A very low tide. You must tell the government lady that you have decided she is right. Right about everything, but that you wish to have a celebration before you leave this house."

"A celebration?"

"Certainly. The night of the fourteenth, to commence at nine p.m. sharp." The little crab began flicking sand across his plate. Leo nodded. "And," the crab continued, "you will invite only the government lady. No one else."

Then the crab explained to him what he must do.

Claudia Brown was surprised to find an envelope wedged between her screen door and its frame. She was even more surprised that it was from Leo, for she was not entirely sure he could write.

The letter read:

Miss Brown: You are rite. Its time. In celebrashun I invite you to a goinaway party at my hous on the fourteen of March at exakly nine p.m. You will be the speshal guest. Leo

She immediately called Vince Gooden to tell him the good news. He told her she must go and then invited her over to his condo to celebrate. It became a good day and a better night for Claudia Brown, the best day and night of her life, and the incident of the talking crab drifted far away into dreamy oblivion.

There was no place for talking crabs in the world of government-imposed real estate deals.

Miss Brown walked to Leo's party a little before nine on the evening of the fourteenth. She had hesitated at the last minute, calling Vince, but he again insisted she go. A smiling Leo answered the door and guided her to the scarred dining table, where he had placed a few mismatched pieces of dinnerware.

"So . . . where are the other guests?" she asked as she seated herself, in the same way one might question a drop of rain on a cloudless day.

"Oh, it's just us," he replied.

She attempted a smile, her upper lip ascending horse-like over her teeth. "I'm so glad you came to your senses, Leo. You'll be much happier in a home. They have puzzles and activities and sing-alongs. Doesn't that sound nice?"

"Sounds wonderful!" Leo nodded and looked at the clock on the mantle.

9:10.

"I'll just go get the food," he said. "We're having crab for dinner." He walked through the kitchen, slipped out the door and locked it, as instructed. He then walked quietly around the house and locked the front door too. Earlier, he had closed all the curtains. As it was low tide, he went for a night walk on the beach.

Miss Brown thought it odd when she heard her host close the kitchen door. When he didn't return she began to tap on her plate with a spoon.

"Leo?" she called. "Leo?"

After a moment she heard little scratching and tapping sounds, which soon swelled into a dozen, then a hundred, then it seemed a thousand scratching tapping sounds like a violent rain on a pond.

She sensed movement behind her and when she turned, she saw them. Thousands of the little creatures. Covering the floor, the furniture, even the walls.

"Crab for dinner," one of them said, and this time she could not deny that she heard it.

Miss Claudia Brown screamed; and when she opened her mouth to scream again she gagged violently as something with many legs fell down her throat.

There was an investigation of course. The missing Miss Brown's entire client base was questioned, including Leo. The police determined she had walked the half-mile to his place from her house, so her car remained where it should be parked, and Leo had taken his nighttime walk to the Poseidon Lounge, where Little Pete the bartender vouched for his presence. No evidence of foul play was ever found (crabs being very thorough), although a few eyebrows were raised when Leo's letter inviting the government worker to his private party turned up among Claudia's things.

Leo claimed he had waited patiently but she never showed. Vince Gooden, who knew where Claudia was supposed to be on that particular night, said nothing, even though it would now take him longer to acquire Leo's house. In the end, he counted it a bit of luck that the woman was gone, for she'd begun to wear on him like a bad shoulder and he was secretly glad to be rid of her.

Another worker was eventually appointed to replace Miss Brown, but she was an older woman awaiting retirement and, to Vince Gooden's irritation, did little aside from sit in the Poseidon Lounge and have a drink or two, or several, every evening.

In the end, Leo kept his house and kept to himself, which was pretty much all he ever wanted. His friendship continued with the little crab and its descendants and friends, though it saddened him to learn that fiddler crabs don't live very long. The throng of crabs were grateful that he had provided such a feast, and because of his kindness, he became a legend among them.

For his part, Leo was happy for their company and had a great many enjoyable conversations with the little creatures, learning many strange and wondrous things, while remaining happily unbothered by government workers.

Blithe

Margie Marek

blithe

—*adjective,* **blith·er, blith·est.**

1. joyous, merry, or happy in disposition; glad; cheerful:
   Everyone loved her for her blithe spirit.
2. without thought or regard; carefree; heedless:
   a blithe indifference to anyone's feelings.

"I should have seen this coming a mile away," Blithe sighed to herself. The discrepancy between the meaning of her name and her current state of emotion was not lost on her.

"Blithe," she sarcastically enunciated out loud to the dragonflies buzzing past her pretty blonde hair and the butterflies alighting on her pink polka-dot dress. The sun reflected its warm light off the edge of the lake, as she sat, pining for her long lost love.

"We reconnected only to be split up once more," her rational mind told her.

"NO!" her emotions countered. "People are all connected! whether or not we see and feel it. He's still there. He still loves us. We must continue to believe."

"False hope," Blithe answered herself aloud. "Like believing in unicorns and leprechauns with their pots of gold at the end of the rainbow."

Another part of her brain combined these two warring factions and spit out a single word in reply

"Faith."

The word did not go down easy. More aptly, she choked on it. Faith got stuck in her throat and formed a lump so big she couldn't swallow. Faith made her angry. Faith had led her to believe in things she couldn't see or rationalize. Faith now came rising up from her stomach and welled up in her eyes, forming rivulets of tears that streamed down her face and dripped their way toward the lake.

The lake swelled with Faith. It surpassed its natural borders and began flooding the town.

Soon, everyone in the town was soaking wet and doused in Faith.

The man that couldn't walk rose up out of his wheelchair and danced a jig.

The blind woman who was born without sight removed her dark glasses and found the world a vision to behold.

The little deaf boy who played by himself, was afraid of his frustration, which came across as meanness and ill-temper, heard a bird chirp for the first time. A wing flap. A breeze pass through his ears. And then he heard his mother's voice.

"Justin," it called out to him, warm and tangible as a kiss. "I love you," it whispered. "Please come home. Dinner is ready."

In no time, Faith filled up the entire town while emptying Blithe of her joylessness.

Faith reminded Blithe why and how she had gotten her name in the first place. Not because of the joy others brought *to* her, but because of the joy inherent *within* her.

"Blithe," she said aloud as she wiped her eyes with the backs of her hands and let free a warm radiant smile to match the setting sun, before buoyantly heading home for dinner.

Strange Impressions

Victor Salia

The Senior Vice President of Corporate Affairs for National Financial Resources, Incorporated lay flat on his back against the tiled men's room floor; his large gray-green eyes stared unblinking at the harsh fluorescence hanging from the ceiling above. His vibrant silver hair - the first gray having begun its invasion at the tender age of twenty-three - was, as always, impeccably groomed in the latest style. He wore a nineteen-hundred-dollar designer suit of imported silk, matching power tie, and Italian leather shoes for which any cow would have been proud to sacrifice her hide.

The man was a true horizontal fashion plate, culled from the pages of *GQ* and *Fortune*. The only disturbing aspect of his attire was the fact that his zipper was down, and his favorite appendage was exposed for all the world to see. Although other men might have found this an extremely uncomfortable position, the Senior Vice President of Corporate Affairs felt no particular shame or embarrassment. In fact, he felt nothing at all.

He was, after all, stone-cold dead.

Homicide detective Lieutenant Dennis Borreigo wiped his ample nose with a moist handkerchief, as he surveyed the crime scene before him. The antihistamine tablets he had been doubling down on for days did little to relieve the allergy attack he always suffered when the Santa Ana winds blew warm dust across the expansive Pacific Ocean, directly into his sinus cavities. Although he was in charge of this investigation, he stood behind the other five police officers, trying to suppress his raging allergies. The uniformed cops were joking with Luther, the building's security guard, about the unfortunate position of the victim's body. They snickered even more when they overheard a secretary outside whisper to her co-workers, "I always thought he'd be bigger than *that...*"

"Let's keep that door closed!" ordered Lt. Borreigo between sneezes. "And throw a towel or somethin' over him. Give the dead guy a break, will ya?"

The assembled cops debated about what they should use to cover the Senior Vice President of Corporate Affairs that would match his expensive outfit. They finally settled on one well-placed paper towel.

Then they had to argue over who was going to place it on him.

"Cut it out, you guys!" Lt. Borreigo barked and sniffled. "This is a crime scene, not a high school locker room!"

A few mumbled apologies were interspersed with a few more unrepentant giggles. The boys in blue were sometimes exactly that. Borreigo turned to Sergeant Frank Caldwell and coughed loudly.

"Looks like a bad cold, Dennis. New haircut, too. Going retro-Beatles, huh?" asked Caldwell.

"Yeah. I meant to sue the barber, but I got called in here instead. And it's these damn allergies, Frank. The Santa Ana winds have it in for me."

"I know what you mean," replied Caldwell, although he didn't.

It was time for Borreigo to get down to business. The sooner he cleared up this mess, the sooner he could get home to a hot lunch of Benadryl, Mucinex and chicken soup.

"What's the victim's name?" he asked. A reasonable first question.

Caldwell ran down the standard data. "Vic's name is Dwight D. Sampson. Forty-four year-old white male. He's a biggie with National Financial Resources down the hall. According to his secretary...he's got three of them, by the way...he left his office to drain the weasel at approximately 10:48 AM. At approximately 11:02, Luther Begley, the building's rent-a-cop, entered the men's room on a similar mission, only to find the victim laid out, uh, thusly…"

"Anyone touch the body since?"

"Um, nobody seemed particularly inclined to," smirked Caldwell.

"You know what I mean," grumbled Lt. Borreigo, as he wiped his nose again. "You guys inventory the pockets?"

"Yeah. No sign of robbery. Full wallet stuffed with gold cards. More than seven hundred in cash. No change. Expensive ring. Rolex watch. Diamond tie tack. Brass comb. Two condoms, unused. Three handkerchiefs, very used. And a half-empty bottle of Dristan. Seems like the Santa Anas got to him, too."

"Poor guy. Any idea what caused the crater on his forehead?" Borreigo gestured to the huge blue and red welt that rose dramatically against the victim's silver hair. The crescent indentation was more than half-an-inch deep.

"It's a beauty, ain't it?"

"Yeah. Is that the only mark?"

"Seems to be. Abrasion on the back of the skull where he hit the floor. Looks like he hit hard, although there's no sign of blood. My guess is that some perp was after the wallet and watch, so he took our guy out with a whack to the forehead. Some blunt object, probably metal. Our man here spins and falls, but the perp gets scared and runs off."

"How far away is the nearest office?"

"About fifteen feet."

"Glass windows facing the hall?"

"Yeah. It's all part of National Financial Resources."

Lt. Borreigo walked slowly around the victim's body, cataloguing each detail. He continued his barrage of questions without looking up at Caldwell.

"Anyone in the office hear sounds of a struggle?"

"No."

"Looks like the Ladies Room shares this wall. Anyone hear anything?"

"Can't find anyone who was using it at the time."

"And nobody in the office or hallway saw anyone enter or leave the bathroom around the time our Mr. Sampson was availing himself of the facilities?"

"No. One of the women saw our boy walk in. Not unusual, 'cause Dwight here was a bit of a studmuffin when it came to the female administrators and interns. But she claims she didn't notice anyone else come out."

Lt. Borreigo squatted down close to the body and examined the strange crescent-shaped bruise on the victim's forehead. "What kind of blunt instrument you figure could make a mark like this?"

"Damned if I know," Sgt. Caldwell squatted on the other side of Dwight D. Sampson's head and examined the mark closely. "Would have to be solid. And real heavy to crack open his skull and make that kind of a dent. The perp musta caught our guy just about to do his business and whacked him pretty hard."

Borreigo sneezed, then chuckled. "Interesting theory, Caldwell. With deductive reasoning like that, you're sure to stay a sergeant clear through the next Ice Age."

"You got a better theory?" Caldwell couldn't hide the rising anger in his voice. "I mean, Lieutenant Borreigo, sir."

"Sure. This guy wasn't murdered."

The other cops muttered their surprise to each other but knew better than to make their opinions known. Caldwell looked at Borreigo for a long moment, then broke into laughter.

"You're right, Dennis. I see what you're getting at... Dwight D. here does a power walk into the Men's Room. Pulls out his weenie, gets depressed at the size of it, so he grabs a lead pipe with a strange shaped knob on the top, and whacks himself on the forehead hard enough to fall dead on the floor. Case closed. I'm surprised I didn't see it myself!"

Borreigo ignored the sarcasm. "Well, you're a little closer to the truth. But you didn't explain what he did with the murder weapon."

Caldwell was on his feet, staring at Borreigo in disbelief.

"How the hell should I know? Maybe he flushed it down the urinal!"

Lieutenant Borreigo stood up and smiled triumphantly. "Now, you're getting somewhere!" he said, then sneezed again.

"I think the Santa Anas are really getting to you, Dennis. If you write this one up as a suicide, they're gonna laugh you off the force."

"I never said it was suicide, Sergeant. I just said that no one murdered him."

One rookie policeman from the other side of the bathroom stepped forward, nervously. "What's the difference, Lieutenant?"

"Twenty-five years to life, patrolman." Borreigo waved the rookie over to his side, and they both bent over the body still sprawled out on the Men's Room floor. "Take a good look at the bruise on his forehead, son."

"Yes, sir." The rookie squinted at the mark carefully, trying to figure out what he was supposed to see in it. He suddenly regretted interrupting the conversation between two superior officers.

Borreigo sensed the young patrolman's discomfort and changed his tone.

"What's your name, son?"

"Murphy. Patrolman Keith Murphy."

"Well, Murphy," continued the older detective. "What angle would you say the weapon that made the mark impacted his skull?"

"Judging by the indentation, sir, I'd say it was a slightly upward angle."

"And where would the perpetrator have to be standing, in order to make such a mark?"

"I'm guessing right in front of the victim, sir."

"Okay, Murphy. Let's assume you are the perpetrator and I am the victim. You're carrying a lead pipe of some kind and sneaking up on me. You have to be real quiet because our vic here has his personality still hanging out, and his clothes and fingernails show absolutely no sign of struggle."

"Uh, okay…"

"So I'm him, standing in front of the urinal, completely unaware of your presence. How are you going to knock me out?"

"I'd just hit you on the head before you had a chance to see me," Murphy grinned. "Of course I'd do it with all the respect accorded a senior officer, sir."

"Of course you would, patrolman. However, the victim was struck from the front, not the back of the head. Tell me how you do that?"

"No problem. I'd grab your shoulder, spin you around and smash your skull with the pipe before he could react."

"So you meant to kill him? This is premeditated murder? Not a robbery?"

"Not necessarily," interjected Caldwell.

"So you plan to commit the murder right here, in the middle of the day? In a busy office with dozens of witnesses that could see you enter and exit the bathroom?"

"But no one did…"

"Then you're either invisible, or a real pro."

Borreigo paused to let that sink in.

"Okay. Let's assume you really are some sort of super ninja assassin. You sneak past all his lusting ladies and all the other office workers. Enter the men's room where you magically know he's all alone and know you have enough time to off our Mr. Sampson without being disturbed…"

"We never said it was premeditated, Dennis…"

"No, you just said the killer offed the guy, then panicked without taking the thousands of dollars in easy pickings off his victim. I don't know many top level assassins, but I'm pretty sure if they have the skill to stalk our victim so perfectly, plus waltz in and out of this building undetected, they probably wouldn't panic once they took him down."

"So maybe it wasn't a hit. Maybe some newbie just planned to rob him and got carried away?"

Borreigo looked at the victim again. "Okay, let's explore that theory. I'm standing facing porcelain and doing my business. You creep in and decide to spin me around to hit me on the forehead. Wouldn't that give me a chance to see your face? Giving your victim a chance to identify you is something no criminal ever wants to do."

"So maybe it wasn't a robbery..." Caldwell interrupted again. "Maybe it was an argument with someone he knew that got out of hand?"

"Someone he knew well enough to leave himself hanging out like a limp flagpole all the time they're arguing? And remember, there was no sign of struggle. The victim was caught completely unawares, so it would have to escalate from harsh words to murder pretty damn quick. Nobody heard shouting, and again, this guy is dangling his participle while trying to make his rebuttals."

Lt. Borreigo moved in front of the urinal. He scrunched up his nose to stop himself from sneezing again, then pretended to unzip his pants.

"Why don't you attack me now, Officer Murphy?"

"Sir?"

"As the perpetrator. Show me how you would hit me."

"Yes, sir."

In semi-slow motion, Murphy pulled out his standard issue nightstick and snuck up on his superior officer, who now stood facing the urinal. Murphy silently raised the black baton over his head, and suddenly spun Borreigo around to face him.

"Stop!" yelled Borreigo, and Murphy froze in position with the raised club poised to smash down upon his victim. "Look at your weapon. What angle are you swinging it?"

"Um...downward, sir," Murphy replied.

"But our victim was hit with an upward thrust. And from straight in front, remember?" Borreigo turned to face the porcelain urinal once more. His eyes watered and he suppressed another sneeze, before calling out to Murphy over his shoulder. "Do it again, son."

Hesitantly, Murphy stepped back a few paces and tried a second time to recreate the attack. He gently spun his victim around to face him, but quickly realized he was now standing much too close. He would have to move back at least two steps to execute an upward thrust with his nightstick. As the rookie officer stepped back, it became clear to everyone crowded into the Men's Room that it would be difficult, if not impossible, to leave the kind of strange mark on the victim's forehead from this angle.

"Okay, so you all see the problem here?" said Borreigo. "Given the amount of time you would need to position yourself to strike at that angle, is it at all conceivable that I, as the victim, would just stand here and watch you?"

"No, sir." Two other policemen's voices joined with Murphy. It was like Detective School 101 in this Pacific Palisades Men's Room, and they realized their puffy-nosed instructor was not half as dumb as they first thought.

"Tell me, Murphy. Do you think you could muster sufficient force with a straight upward thrust to knock me out, much less cave in my skull, if I'm standing like this?"

"No, sir."

Borreigo bent forward at the waist, so that his forehead was positioned directly over Murphy's nightstick.

"Do you think you could deliver enough upward force to crack my forehead, if I was standing this way?"

Murphy smiled. "Now that would be no problem at all, sir."

"Try not to enjoy the image too much, patrolman."

"Yes, sir. I mean, no, sir. Sorry, sir."

"It's okay, Officer Murphy. You're doing fine." The lead detective bent forward again. "Now, do you think it is conceivable that our VP Of Fashion here would obligingly place himself in this position with a robber, a killer, or someone he's arguing with?"

Murphy's face fell. "Not unless he was trying to do something kind of, um...kinky...sir."

"Okay, let's run with that for a moment. Is it likely our boy with a private office and a reputation for being a studmuffin would risk engaging in a somewhat unconventional sexual act in the middle of an open Men's Room only fifteen feet from said office? Or to be so friendly with someone who happens to be holding a large metal pipe at the time?"

It was Frank Caldwell who responded this time. "Pretty doubtful. Unless he got off on the thrill of being caught in the act." Then he smiled and added, "...sir."

"Well, let's assume it happened this way, just for the sake of physics." Borreigo stifled another sneeze, then bent over and acted out the scene as he described it. "Our kinkmaster bends over in the middle of his office Men's Room, for reasons known only to him and his therapist. His assailant, Grinder date, or best friend, says hi, then somehow makes a heavy piece of metal appear out of nowhere to deliver a smashing upward blow to the face. I'm him. You hit me hard. How does my head go?"

"It snaps backward, sir."

"Correct, probably hitting the back of my head on the urinal, even though there is no similar indentation on the back of the victim's skull. Anyway, from there, how do I fall?"

Luther, the security guard, was the first to answer.

"Your knees would buckle, and you'd crash face first, like some kinda dead tree."

Borreigo smiled. "Good answer. My arms would probably be thrown back, too. And, even if I were to spin around as I fell, there is no way I could logically land in the position that we find our victim in now. Flat on my back. Undisturbed clothing. Arms by my side. Straight legged. The top of my head facing the door."

"Could the murderer have moved the body?" Luther was really feeling like one of the boys in blue now. "Y'know, so we wouldn't be able to figure it out?"

"You mean, the *alleged* murderer? Who committed our *alleged* murder?" Borreigo corrected him. "Are you asking us whether the alleged murderer smashed a man's skull, then calmly repositioned his body, ignoring wallet, watch and jewelry, and then left the victim dangling like that?"

"I dunno. I guess that's what I'm asking."

Now it was Caldwell's turn to interrupt again.

"Okay, Lieutenant. You've walked us through all the ways and the reasons this could not possibly have happened. But you haven't given us any explanation of how you think it actually did happen. So what are we left with here?"

"Well, the murder weapons for one thing. They are right in front of your eyes." The sudden tumult of confusion in the room was interrupted when the door opened and a small, thin man with glasses entered. He stared, wide-eyed, at the dead body and the throng of frustrated policemen, then quickly decided to use a Men's Room on a different floor. By the time the bathroom door swung closed again, Borreigo knew he could not drag the suspense out any longer. No matter how much he enjoyed doing so. He squatted down and pointed to the victim's pocket.

"You all overlooked the most obvious clue. His handkerchiefs."

A third uniformed cop, Officer Shimazu, spoke first. "You lost us, sir."

"Look. Three very moist handkerchiefs and a bottle of Dristan allergy medication. The guy had severe allergies!"

By this point, Caldwell was considering murdering his lead detective, no matter how it might hinder his career advancement.

"Dennis, please... Just tell us where the hell this supposed murder weapon is supposed to be!"

"Just where you said it would be, Frank. In the urinal."

The officers rushed forward as a group, but all they saw was a large chunk of pink chlorine in the basin of the urinal. Borreigo turned to Luther.

"Luther, is this the same type of solid disinfectant they've always used in this building?"

"I don't think so. The last stuff was white. Didn't smell as bad."

"What are you saying, Dennis? A urinal cake killed our executive?"

"Damn it, Frank! He had allergies! I've been sneezing my head off since I walked into this Men's Room. I thought it was the Santa Ana winds, but it's worse in here than outside! That perfumed hunk of chlorine is killer to a sensitive nose. Luther, can you tell me whether Mr. Sampson was a big sneezer?"

"Mr. Sampson? That dude could blow over a house with just his nostrils!"

That was all he needed to hear. Lt. Borreigo decided it was time to act out the last seconds of Senior Vice President Dwight D. Sampson's life.

"It's 10:48 AM. Our boy here has a sensitive nose and a full bladder. He walks calmly into this porcelain palace. Pulls down his zipper and stands in front of this urinal. Suddenly, he gets a strong whiff of that new chunk of pink chlorine and he..."

"Sneezes!" Murphy yelled with excitement.

"That's right. Our Mr. Perfect sneezes so hard, it snaps his head forward, smashing his forehead on this chrome fixture on top of the urinal."

"Death by urinal? You gotta be kidding me?!"

"Unfortunately for Sneezy Sampson here, I'm not. Notice the crescent shape on the top of this urinal fixture? It perfectly matches the mark on his forehead. His head is propelled downward, giving the impression…excuse the pun…of a blunt object's upward thrust. If he hits hard enough to crack his skull, his head snaps backwards, and he would fall to the exact position we find his body in now."

The stunned officers all looked at the victim and the killer porcelain fixture with awe. Only Caldwell was shaking his head.

"C'mon, Dennis. You expect us to believe this high-powered boy wonder sneezed himself to death?"

"That's right. And if you were observant enough to examine the top of this urinal here, you'll find a small amount of skin scrapings, plus a strand of silver hair that looks suspiciously close to the victim's color."

Murphy looked up at Borreigo with wonder. "How'd you even think of something like that?" he asked.

"It's a gift," Borreigo smiled wryly, then looked down at the victim and shook his head.

"If Mr. VP had felt the urge to sit instead of stand...our boy would probably be alive today."

Back home, a few hours later, Homicide Detective Lieutenant Dennis Borreigo was wearily drying his hands in front of his bathroom sink. He carefully inspected his face in the mirror and grimaced at the dark, swollen circles his allergies had puffed out under his eyes. Then he leaned closer and brushed the straight tufts of brown hair off his forehead. He examined the painful, slightly bluish crescent mark, which he got two days ago, but had yet to fade away.

Borreigo brushed his hair down over the bruise again, then left the bathroom in search of more antihistamines.

Beyond The Sea

Ross Tuohy

The softly soothing seas rocked the small blue ship to and fro, as the Sailor leaned against the rudder adjusting his course by a few lazy degrees. Seabirds called out, wheeling above him in easy flight as their outstretched wings caught the thermals. Their silhouettes crossed the sun and the Sailor marveled at the way the bright rays transformed their wings into translucent pastel rainbows.

He tasted salt on the air and smiled, staring out at an endless expanse of sapphire water which popped and flashed with silver coins of light as the waves rose and fell. The sails fluttered in the wind like sheets on a line and the Sailor paused to listen. He always listened to his ship, and though the journey had been longer than he had expected, and in some places arduous, he found his ship would never steer him wrong if he took the time to listen to it. The flutter of the sails whispered to him, divining the quickest route he needed to take. The squeak of the rudder had brought him through many treacherous reefs with nothing more than a few superficial scrapes. and the bowsprit often became a dousing rod for treasure.

His little blue ship often came home with its hold groaning with gold and silver. A storm had swallowed his map a week ago, but he didn't care. He would find his way home soon enough.

The sun danced along his skin with pleasant warm prickling sensation as he flexed his calloused fingers against the rudderpost. He raised a hand to his eyes, shielding them from the sun's golden glare and scanned the horizon again, finding nothing but blue. He thought for a moment, tying off the rudder to keep his course true and moved over to the starboard railing. He dipped a scarred and calloused hand into a large wooden crate, fishing around until his thick fingers seized a collapsible brass spyglass. He unfurled a small lace handkerchief from his coat pocket, letting the breeze play along its length before scrubbing a thin layer of blue-grey grime from the lens. He carefully eased the sections apart and placed the spyglass to his eye, but the retreating horizon revealed nothing but water.

Off in the distance, a gathering of seabirds circled a small patch of sea, folding their wings to their bodies and zipping into the waves like feathered torpedoes. Bright orange beaks slashed upwards through the water, silver fish tails twitching from each side. The birds returned to the skies, gulping down their meals with their wet wings that sent sparkling diamonds swirling through the air.

The Sailor's heart fell, as he turned his eye from the spectacle. No hazy black mountains crouched over the waves to greet him. No familiar coastline held the promise of rest and comfort. Despite his eternal faith in his vessel, pangs of worry began to prod at his heart. Could he remember the course he'd set all that time ago? Could he draw a new map if he needed it? Would he ever end up where he wanted to be? As the questions gnawed at the edges of his mind he took a hesitant but determined breath, craning his head upwards to let the warming sun kiss his face, the spyglass trailing in the loose grip of his left hand.

He stood like this for a time, heat toasting the tip of his nose, and listening to the waves sigh against the hull of his faithful ship. The little blue vessel would put his worries to rest as it always did. All he had to do was listen.

And listen he did.

He focused his ears on the whisper of the waves softly slapping the old wooden hull. He heard the ropes sway in a gentle rhythm, the block and tackle clinking against them, twanging out a low discordant tune like slack violin strings. The waves sloshed and the birds cried, and he listened to the soothing song of the sea.

He opened his eyes a fraction, squinting at the blurred spear of the bowsprit and waited. He sailed on, even as the cooling sun began its evening descent, staining the wisps of clouds in liquid gold, which faded into the deep grapefruit pink of dusk. The Sailor yawned and stretched, content as the the sun crawled closer to the horizon. As the yellow disk kissed the blue water, it suddenly erupted into a huge ball of phosphorescent green flame, which surged and spread along the waves. The small ship lurched to starboard as the wall of green fire burst against its port side. The Sailor threw himself towards the railing as panic seized his heart. He stared down at the side of the ship dumbfounded. Where flames should have been devouring the wood, only small patches of luminous green sparkled in the fading light, releasing tufts of jade smoke which snaked through the rising air. Light grey clouds began to roll in. Shifting mists of emerald smoke shrouded the disappearing sun in reversed rivulets of silver and green. A sudden rain turned the sea ashen. Fat droplets buffeted the sailcloth sliding down the lines and painting them black. The spars groaned as the wind whistled and the rain beat an angry rat-a-tat on the deck. The sodden cloth slapped against the wind, as yet another thin layer of mist began to rise from the water. The rain increased in ferocity, slashing down in summer sheets. The Sailor lunged forward, seizing the rudderpost to keep its flailing line from dancing a jig across the deck. The strange storm grew more violent. The sea began to roil. Green mists were chased off by white foam bubbling up from the depths. Great grey waves broke against the prow, showering the Sailor in icy salt spray. He coughed out a mist of terror as more waves slammed and battered and propelled his little ship forward, its dancing prow splitting the water like an arrow. Thunder growled overhead and the drumbeat of the rain quickened into a constant roar. A howl of wind ballooned the mainsail, the spars screamed, and the Sailor was hurled forward once again. The ship pitched wildly, splinters racing up the main mast like cracks on a frozen pond. Sheets of white light sparked and popped in the sky as the clouds turned a furious grey. Another massive wave loomed over the horizon, as a long blueish-purple fork of lightning split the sky, striking the water with a hammer blow of pure fury.

The pelting rain coursed down the Sailor's face, turning the world before him into frosted glass. His shirt became a second skin weighted down by sea and rain. A curtain of numbing water cascaded down his back, along his legs and into his boots, which squelched as he lumbered from one end of the ship to the other, snatching at anything that might hold the boat together. The mast roared in pain as the wind began to wrench it apart. The wood buckled under the weight of sodden rope and tattered sailcloth.

There was nothing to do but surrender to the chaos.

The Sailor took one more freezing breath, closed his eyes, released the rudder and waited for the end to come.

But there was only silence.

No screaming ship. No howling wind. No relentless hiss of rain. He kept his eyes shut, fearing the peaceful illusion more than the enraged storm, yet the sound of the waves was now as calm and gentle as it had been all morning. Still quaking with fear, he chanced a look. The clouds had vanished and all above him was a fathomless royal blue sky with the fat golden doubloon of the sun hanging overhead. He cast his eye around the ship in wonder. The mainmast was not bent or broken but stood proud and tall as the pristine white sails flapped in a soft, warm breeze. The deck was dry, the dark wood shimmering as if it had been lacquered with a fresh coat of varnish. The ropes swung gently in the whispery wind, dry as the day they were first woven. The water gleamed a simple unbroken blue, a world of blown glass that his reborn ship now glided across without so much as a nudge of the rudder.

Something peeked over the horizon and the Sailor seized his spyglass. Misty points of verdant mountains greeted his eye and he yelped with joy, scattering the gulls that executed lazy circles overhead. The Sailor roped the rudder back into position and set course for land. As the small ship skipped along the ocean, the surface of the sea began to fade from deepest blue to a clear silver so perfect, he could spy a school of fish dance below, scales shimmering in iridescent greens and purples. He laughed as the fish twisted in the water, swimming in perfect unison to the course he set.

The mountains shouldered their way out of the sea, with peaks shimmering like cut emeralds. The resurgent sun warmed the Sailor's back and the breeze caressed his cheeks as the water beneath him began to change again darkening to a vivid clover green. He leaned over the port side, trailing his fingers in water that felt as if it had been drawn from a warm bath. A pleasant tingling scurried up his arm, along his shoulder and down his neck. It blossomed as it fell into his stomach sending a warm radiance throughout his body, which massaged his aching muscles. He sighed, blissfully content as his hand trailed lazy patterns in the water and his fingertips brushed the smooth scales of the occasionally curious fish.

As his island drew closer, soft fiddle music began to drift through the air. The Sailor drummed the fingers of his free hand in time with the merry tune, as the purity and serenity of his new surroundings took hold. A soft smile played across his lips as his ship came to at the edge of a pristine, white sand beach, which stretched out beyond his eyes, as if a thousand hourglasses had been shattered, spilling centuries into every crevice of the rocks. Lush green hills covered the island, long shards of grass dancing in the breeze. Dazzling birds of paradise nested in stout trees, their tail feathers trailing behind them like a welcome banner as they took flight and swirled through the air.

The Sailor swung his weary legs over the bow of his small ship, waded through the surf and threw himself down on the warm sand. He let his eyes follow the mast of the ship until they reached the blazing sun. He was surprised there was no glare, even when he stared straight into its golden depths, just a cleansing warmth that made his heart ache with joy. His sudden laughter merged with the soft serenade of the island, and crossed his legs, tapping the toe of his left boot to the heel of his right in time with the gentle tune.

"Welcome home," he whispered as he drifted off in waves of peaceful slumber.

Could I? Should I? Would I?

Mandy Morreale

Michelle Miller sat nervously at the table. She was dressed in all black, right down to the oversized sunglasses that consumed the majority of her face while successfully hiding her presumably tear-soaked eyes. Tear-soaked, because her husband had just passed away the day before, and now she soothed herself by tapping her long, manicured nails on the table.

Tap. Tap. Tap.

Tap. Tap. Tap…

Followed again by an even quicker…

Tap. Tap. Tap.

Then silence.

Minutes passed without a word being spoken.

And then…

Tap. Tap. Tap.

The tapping had no pattern, no rhythm or reason, as if she was trying to translate her emotions into Morse code. It wasn't until she chipped the tip of her fingernail before she spoke.

"Damn it! I knew I should've paid extra and gotten the gel polish. They always want to charge you an extra ten dollars, saying it will last longer, but no, I didn't do it this time…"

Michelle turned her finger over to closely examine it and tried to smooth the polish as best she could.

"That's forty bucks wasted. Ruined that fast! I mean I *could* have gotten the gel polish. I *should* have just spent the extra ten bucks. I *would* have too, but he has been complaining about my spending lately, so I tried to tone it down some."

Michelle sighed out loud.

"That seems to be the story of my life. It always comes down to those same three questions... Could I? Should I? Would I?" She searched the other woman's face for sympathy, or at least some degree of understanding. Seeing little, she pushed harder. "Ever since high school, really. And every decision I've made since. Almost like a moral pros and cons list."

Michelle began tapping again, this time with the opposite hand.

"I even remember the moment these questions first consumed me, you know? I was just a teenager, running through the hallway at school on my way to class. I remember very carefully keeping my distance behind Jon Wellman. Jon was the biggest bully in the school, and for some unknown reason, he felt it was his mission to torment me daily. He was only a few feet in front of me, and he reached into his back pocket to pull out a piece of paper that he handed to Lydia, the airhead cheerleader always hanging on his arm. Neither of them noticed, but Jon dropped a twenty dollar bill on the floor as he pulled the note out to give Lydia. This was where it began, an internal ethical interrogation. Could I casually bend down and pick up that $20? I mean, I knew that no one would notice. No one would see me pick it up or be able to prove it wasn't mine. So I *could* do that. But should I? Jon was an asshole, especially to me, and Lydia wasn't much better. They had been tormenting me since grade school. So yes, I *should* take his money just to teach them both a lesson. But that would have made me no better than him. I wasn't that type of person. I don't steal, and if I had dropped my money and someone saw I'd definitely want them to tell me.

"I just stood there staring at that unclaimed twenty-dollar bill, then looked up at those two privileged assholes laughing at all the other students they considered below them. I bent down and casually picked up the $20. I didn't have it in my hand more than five seconds before I had to answer the final questions. Would I keep it? I learned at that moment that *Would I?* is always the hardest question, when your morality moves from the theoretical to the point when you come face-to-face with the best or worst of yourself.

"So I shouted out "Hey Jon," and he turned around and shot me a look of pure disgust.

"What do you want?" he snapped at me. 'Why are you even talking to me, loser?"

"At that moment I felt three inches tall, and even though I tried not to show it, I couldn't help my eyes from filling up with tears. Everyone in the hall turned and stared, wondering the same thing. Who was I to talk to Jon Wellman, high school royalty?

"I reached out a trembled hand toward him, afraid to even make eye contact.

"You dropped this," I mumbled, the twenty-dollar bill crumpled in my fingers. He looked at me with surprise, then quickly felt around in his back pocket. Then he snatched the money out of my hand, turned and walked away. No 'thank you.' No sign of appreciation at all. I was honest but I was still a loser in his eyes.

"In that moment, I decided the next time I was presented with an opportunity to get even with someone who treated me in a way

I didn't deserve, I knew what the answer to my *Would I?* question would be from now on."

The faraway look that haunted Michelle Miller while telling her story slowly faded. She glanced up at the woman sitting across from her with an embarrassed smile, then resumed tapping her fingers on the table. When the other woman remained silent, Michelle stopped tapping and began picking at her peeling nail polish with her teeth. A small chip of passion pink came off, and she spit it on the table, before covering it with her hands.

"Isn't it odd that something as simple and silly as a high school bully dropping a twenty-dollar bill had such a profound effect on my life? It makes you wonder if either saints or serial killers are able to pinpoint the exact moment they changed?"

More silence.

Michelle took a deep, staccato breath before she went back to biting the polish off her now destroyed manicure.

"Not that I'm a saint or a serial killer. I'm not admitting to anything. Just thinking out loud, you know? I mean do I look like the type of person who could murder someone? I mean of course I *could*, of course. Anyone *could*, but I had no reason to. It's not something that I should have done or even would have done. He was my husband! I loved him. I still love him. I'll always love him!"

Michelle lifted her sunglasses and pushed them on top of her head to hold her hair back. Her eyes darted about the room, then up to the video camera suspended from the ceiling in the far corner. The other woman facing her wrote something in her notepad.

Makeup intact. Not a single smudge in her mascara.

"Tell me more about your husband." The woman's voice was calm. Controlled.

Michelle nodded and continued.

"The day he asked me to marry him, I had the same internal interrogation you know? *Could I* do this? Could I see myself being with this man every single day for the rest of his life? The rest of my life, I mean. I knew the answer was 'of course, I could. *Should I* marry him? He's been wonderful, as long as I've known him, and I had no doubt he loves me. So yes, I should marry him. But *would I?* After all the chaos and disappointments in my life, would I chicken out and cause a fight right before we were supposed to walk down the aisle, just so he would have an excuse to call the whole thing off? I mean, I confess that did go through my mind at the time, but no, I wouldn't do that. Not to him. Not this time. I loved him. I could, I should, and I would marry him. And that's exactly what I did. Because I loved him. So how anyone could think I had anything to do with what happened is beyond me."

Michelle looked around the room, scanned the other woman's face one more time, then repositioned herself in her chair and placed the sunglasses back on her face.

"He snores, you know. I mean, snores like a squirrel trapped in a woodchipper. It was terrible. I couldn't sleep all night. You can't imagine what that does to a person…"

Michelle coughed, looked to the wall, then adjusted herself again.

"And it was his fault that he snored!" she blurted out. "If he would have just gone to bed at a reasonable time, you know, like a normal person, he probably wouldn't snore so bad! Or he wouldn't *have* snored so bad."

She found another flaw in her nails and began to chew on them again. "But he would stay up all night, sometimes for days at a time, pounding away on whatever project he was currently working on. Then he would take three or four sleeping pills and chase them down with a big swig of Nyquil. Which, by the way, he would always leave sitting on the bathroom sink, so it left a sticky colored ring I would have to clean up in the morning. The sticky ring wasn't as bad as the toothpaste I'd have to scrub off the mirror. I mean, how do you splatter the mirror with toothpaste like that? And is it so much to ask that someone just wipe it off when they make a mess like that? You know what I'm saying?"

But the other woman's expression was unreadable, and Michelle Miller began to think, *Maybe I shouldn't say as much?* Her eyes again darted around the room and rested on the doorway. Could she just get up and leave? Should she? Would she?

Instead she crossed her arms over her chest and let the silence once again fill the room. But the amount of it suffocated her, and she continued in a softer voice.

"Could I have placed a pillow over his head any night he was under the influence of one of his insomnia cocktails? Sure, I *could* have. *Should* I have done it? I mean, probably. I lost many hours of sleep listening to that, but *would I?* No! I wouldn't do that. I miss the sound of that snore now. I can't tell you how much. I'd give anything to hear that snore again. I really would!"

She gazed up at the lights. They were bright and hot, and causing her to perspire the longer this went on.

:"You know he was a hoarder too. He kept everything! I mean everything. He would take home unused paper napkins from restaurants! The glovebox, his dresser and a couple of our kitchen drawers were full of napkins. Napkins and receipts I can't forget about those receipts. What did we need all those receipts for? Doesn't he know everything is electronic these days? You can see your bank statements and every credit card transaction on your phone anytime you want! Why on earth does anyone need drawers and drawers of receipts, some going back years!"

Michelle stared at her empty coffee cup. Her manicure was all but gone and tiny chips of passion pink polish littered the table. The coffee cup reminded her of something else he used to do.

"He always drank his coffee black, no sugar. I don't know why. He hated the taste of it but liked to say it was healthier that way. I mean, why even drink coffee at all if you're going to drink it black? But I never said anything. I just let him talk and tried to keep him happy. That's why I moved his ridiculous sword collection into the bedroom. Just to make him happy. He loved those damn things. He would have had them hanging in every room of the house, if I would have allowed it. But talk about tacky… Who wants Viking swords hanging in their living room? Who needs a genuine samurai sword and a Game of Thrones replica dagger next to the toaster? But to make him happy, just to make him happy, I let him move them to the bedroom. I even bought him a special mount and let him hang them up above the bed. Yes, I might have been the one to suggest that but, but we had a special mount, and it's not my fault that he didn't install it correctly, is it? I *could have* been a nagging wife and make him sell the stupid things off. I could have insisted he hide them away in a closet or maybe a storage unit somewhere. That's what I *should have* done. And truthfully, I wish I had. But I let him have his swords and his napkins and his receipts and his black coffee… Because that's what a good wife *would* do!

Michelle attempted to stand, but she could only move so far with the shackles attached to the table.

"Can you take these handcuffs off me now, please?" she asked the woman with the notepad. "I've told you everything I can about the accident. And I have things to do. I am a grieving widow with a funeral to plan."

Lieutenant Detective Belinda Warren rose from the table and looked down at Michelle.

"Mrs. Miller, can you explain to me how your fingerprints were found on the handles of all seventeen swords, yet you have repeatedly stated that your husband was the one who hung them in the bedroom by himself? And while I could let you slide on that little piece of evidence, because you do live in the home as well, and a jury might assume that you probably touched every sword your husband owned at one point or other."

"I do polish them occasionally. It made my husband so happy to see them shine."

"I'm sure it does. But what's a mystery to all of us here at the LMPD is how all seventeen blades were standing upright, while wedged inside his body? Our forensics team has examined the mounts you say were incorrectly installed, yet they find it nearly impossible that all seventeen swords fell from that placement with enough force to penetrate six inches into his chest and abdomen. Not a single one even touched the mattress, not to mention the complete disruption of the law of physics and geometry that enabled all seventeen blades to miss you entirely, though you were claimed to have been sleeping right beside him at the time of the…um, accident."

Michelle Miller didn't like what the other woman was implying. And she definitely didn't like the way Lieutenant Detective Warren leaned in, uncomfortably close to her ear.

"But what we can't let slide is the twenty-seven receipts our team removed from husband's throat when they performed the autopsy. Or the traces of rat poison that were found in his coffee cup by the bed, as well as in the Nyquil bottle under the bathroom sink..."

Lieutenant Warren leaned back with a smile cold and harsh as week-old coffee.

"So, Mrs. Miller," she continued. "*Could I* take your handcuffs off? Yes ma'am, I could. *Should I* take your handcuffs off? No ma'am I shouldn't. Not with all the evidence that points to you as the main suspect in this questionable death. But finally, *would I?*'

The detective leaned in close and whispered in Michelle's ear. "What kind of screwed-up moral code would I have to have, if I were to accidentally drop this handcuff key on the table, and then head out for a bathroom break that might last, oh, I don't know… maybe just long enough for a potential suspect to make it out that door, then down the hallway to the left, and out to the back parking lot?"

The detective shook her head, as she turned and walked out of the interrogation room.

"Just so you know," she said, forgetting to lock the door behind her. "I've been married twenty-nine years, and my husband snores like a squirrel in a woodchipper too…"

Gills

Gary Wadley

Sandy had gills.

That's what she called the sagging skin at her jaw line and on her neck. Or maybe she had a wattle? Was it better to be a fish or a bird? She couldn't decide. She looked into the bathroom mirror, curled her lips into a smile, shook her head and watched the loose skin on her neck wobble from side to side.

"Okay," she said. "I'm not a girl anymore." The truth is, she hadn't been a girl for a long time. Decades. The wrapping was frayed, eyes crinkled, boobs and butt gone south. Disgusting word, she thought, *gills*. Just what every woman wants: *gills*. Probably even fish did not like gills, would prefer a plain old chin, a young neck. She reminded herself to look up the word and started to apply her lipstick.

The kettle's whistle pierced the quiet as she went into the kitchen to make coffee. *This is a nice house that Edd's insurance purchased.* Outside the window, the Gulf of Mexico was pewter, doubling the gray clouds that drifted like puffy ships toward the mainland. A few lazy gulls sat on her decomposing dock, facing the breeze that was beginning to stir whitecaps.

Then she saw him and smiled. Bobby had returned, poling his skiff from boat to dock, the stern full of net and tubs of mullet sitting in the bottom. A dance, she thought, watching him move lightly from bow to stern, pushing the long pole along the side of the skiff, stepping on whatever surface was available. A misstep would send him into the water or maybe even break a leg. She could not understand how he kept the boat going straight when he pushed from the side.

At first it had surprised her that she looked for him to come and go with the tide; it was not like her. (What *was* like her anymore?) She'd started to watch him almost as soon as she'd moved to the island, even checking the tide chart everyday so she could calculate his comings and goings. She saw how the Gulf light defined the muscles of his arms, like ropes that pulled and slackened as he poled the boat, his face hidden beneath a floppy straw hat and dark glasses. Miss Poteet, the widow fishwife, had told her how the fishermen tried to hide from the sun, fought it as much as the wind, its potency magnified by reflection from the water, coming at a man from two directions with cancer and cataracts. Curious, Sandy thought, the man had the same name as her son, though her son had always insisted on being called Robert, even as a child.

Turning from the window, she pulled the heavy old dictionary from its shelf, laid it on the table and flipped through the dog-eared pages.

Gill: *a respiratory organ found in many aquatic organisms that extracts dissolved oxygen from water, afterward excreting carbon dioxide.*

She touched the flesh beneath her chin.

In the bathroom she practiced jutting and lifting her head, trying to lessen the neck lines, but it only made her appear demented. She gave up and curled and fluffed her hair, then trimmed her bangs to more-or-less even.

"Gills," she said, "the calling card of gravity."

She pulled on dark slacks and a cream blouse, hesitated, then put on the pair of pearl earrings Edd had given her. She'd worn them every day since his passing, beginning with the funeral. Each time she put them on she offered up a prayer.

He was *there*, going to make a pot of coffee one Sunday morning just as he had every Sunday morning for years, and then he'd flopped down like a blanket thrown across the floor and now he was *not there* anymore. Thirty-five years of marriage concluded by a blockage smaller than a pea.

It was Friday evening and she thought she'd walk down to the Poseidon Bar to listen to Guitar Joe play one of the two songs he knew, M*argaritaville* or *Sweet Home Alabama* (which he called *Sweet Home Cedar Key*). She laughed, thinking it funny that she was taking her gills to the Poseidon Bar. She must look him up someday, this formidable god of the sea.

She rinsed her cup in the sink and looked toward Seahorse, the island across the bay. She could just see a spot of white, the old lighthouse. Out from the beach, Bobby's skiff was tied at his old boat house and he was gone.

There was a knock at the door. "Just a minute," she called touching a finger to her bangs. She opened the door to find Bobby standing there with a wrapped newspaper package in his hand. Sandy opened her mouth, but nothing came out.

"Hello, Sandy," he said and waved the package at her. "I thought you might like some mullet." He held the fish out as if they were delicate things, some sort of offering. He had never come to her house before. She had never invited him -- had not been able to.

She took the fish. "Why, thank you," she said, smiling and trying to look casual. Though he was on the stoop and she was in the doorway she could smell him, salt and sweat and fish and honest work, and she remembered how her father had smelled when she ran into his arms after he came home from work at the factory.

She thought again of Poseidon.

His brown eyes flickered and looked away. "You look nice," he said, as if he were remarking on the weather or the color of the sky. She felt herself blush. Didn't he see she was fat and old? That she had *gills*?

"Thank you," she said. "I saw you come in and wondered..." He smiled and looked at her. "...wondered if you'd had any luck?"

"A little," he said. "You never really know, with luck or with fish. You can't count on either one."

She wanted to say something profound, then remembered she'd only put lipstick on her top lip.

How surprised he'd be if he knew she looked for his boat, that she looked for him to go out or come in each and every day, that she knew exactly where and when he sat two pews behind her in the little Baptist church she'd started attending. Did he know that she suspected he might be staring at her in church? At first this alarmed her (they were, after all, in church), but the thought of him sitting behind her and watching her had given her an anticipation and giddy pleasure she hadn't known for years. And, as usual, with the pleasure came guilt. Of course, she couldn't really be sure he was watching her; he was behind her, after all. Maybe it was just an old woman's imagination, but it was pleasurable, and she enjoyed it, and it delighted her that she was able to enjoy anything again. Still, everything always ended up mixed with the memory of Edd.

"Sandy?" It was Bobby's voice. "You okay?"

She nodded. "Getting old, I guess." She looked at the wrapped fish in her hand. An outboard motor gargled somewhere out on the Gulf. *Don't tell him you're old, stupid! He can see you're old!*

Bobby smiled. There was a pause, one of those little moments filled with possibility or with nothing. "Well, I guess I'd better get the catch to the fish house." He pointed to his gift. "Those will fry up real well. I've already cleaned 'em for you. Guess I'll see you in church." Then he nodded and walked off toward the beach.

Ask him, she scolded herself. *Ask him to come for dinner, then maybe a walk around the Big Dock. Maybe a sit and chat in the bar. That's why he brought the fish, you big dummy. You've already got yourself dressed.* But she said nothing, merely stood silent as a channel marker and watched him disappear down the beach.

In the kitchen she unwrapped the fish and found four pearly fillets. Edd had enjoyed fishing, but she was unfamiliar with the saltwater kind, which seemed to overpower their freshwater kin, just as the ocean overpowered the lake - deep, mysterious and dangerous. Who really knew all that the ocean held? Like Cedar Key, she thought, salt air and mud eased into your pores, ready or not. It surprised her when tears came. She held them back until her eyes glistened.

That evening, Sandy sat in the Poseidon Bar sipping sherry. She wasn't really a drinker but had found she liked the sweetness of wine braced with brandy. Actually, that was a lie she liked to tell herself. She used to drink a great deal until she met Edd and settled into big girl life. She sat at the bar because she felt sitting at a table was a signal that she wanted company. The bar proper was made for the single person and that's what she was.

The bar occupied half the ground floor of the Sandbar Hotel, a building from the 1840s that had served as everything from a store to soldiers' quarters to a house of ill repute. Or so it was said. The building had gone through a succession of owners, each adding or detracting as they thought best, until it had evolved into a hotel. The other half of the first floor was a lobby, restaurant and kitchen. The rooms were upstairs and looked untouched from an earlier and simpler time.

Sandy studied the painting behind the bar; Poseidon goofing off with two mermaids. The mermaids appeared delighted to be in the god's presence and she couldn't help but notice that Poseidon did look a little like Bobby, or Bobby looked a little like old Poseidon…minus the beard and long hair.

Of course, the mermaids were topless, half-human and half-fish, and Sandy wondered how they peed, how they bred, and why she was thinking so logically about mythological creatures. But she knew mermaids existed because she had seen one - the one and only time she and Edd had come to Cedar Key all those years ago – out in the channel while they dined at one of the dockside restaurants.

"Another drink?" asked Little Pete. He stood on skids behind the bar and looked up at her.

She shook her head. One was enough, though she knew she was only fooling herself. "Have you ever seen a mermaid, Pete?"

"I seen sea cows. Never a mermaid."

She laughed. She was becoming a sea cow. "I mean, do you think they exist?" The sherry warmed her.

"'*There are more things in heaven and earth,*'" he answered with a grin. Little Pete liked to quote things.

"What . . . ?"

"*There are more things in heaven and earth, Horatio, than are dreamt of in your philosophy.*" Hamlet said that to his friend after they saw his father's ghost. So yeah, I guess there could be mermaids." He looked up at her and scratched behind his ear. "You been seeing mermaids, Sandy?"

"Yep," she answered truthfully, the first time she'd told anyone besides Edd. She resumed studying the painting behind the bar and thought she saw Poseidon wink at her.

"You're doing what?" Robert had asked, back when they sat in her tiny kitchen in Pennsylvania.

"Moving to Florida. To a little island called Cedar Key."

"Where Hemingway lived?" Her son frowned and took a slow sip of coffee.

What lovely eyes, she thought, *his father's eyes*. "No. That's Key West. Cedar Key is a small island in the Gulf where there are no stop lights and very few stop signs. Travis McGee – that sort of thing."

"Travis who?"

"Never mind. I forgot how young you are."

"You know Key West is full of crime, Mom."

He was being obtuse. "No, dear. *Cedar* Key. Your Dad and I stayed there once after a business trip to Orlando." She didn't tell him what she had seen there. She'd never told anyone except Edd. But Edd hadn't laughed and that surprised her. She'd kept the memory tucked away, like a photo in the back of a drawer, comforted to know it was there and that she could take it out anytime she wanted. She could not explain to Robert how the thought of moving, even though it frightened her, had begun to grow on her. A dream that solidified a little each day. A dream of someplace new and fresh and clean of memories (well, not all memories), where every object, every wall and corner did not remind her of the life she no longer possessed. A life that had slipped away from her. She really couldn't even explain it to herself.

Robert wrinkled his nose as though he'd caught a bad smell, then rose and took his cup to the sink and rinsed it. "What's there?" he asked.

Something calling me, she thought, but instead said, "Not much of anything as far as I remember…Mostly water and slow, I believe."

"Slow is not a noun, Mom."

"Maybe it shouldn't be." She knew where the conversation was going, about leaving friends and family and all that was familiar, and at her age…but that was not a concern anymore. She wasn't going to another country, was she? She could always visit, could always return to the safety of the familiar. She took her own cup to the sink and stood next to her son. "You can rent out the condo or sell it," she explained, waving her hand around the room like a real estate agent. "Indoor toilet. Hot water. Electricity."

He fake-laughed.

"Very funny."

She looked up at him over her glasses. "I'm quite serious, young man. It's time for a fresh start. And I'm tired of snow. That's why old folks move to Florida, you know."

He considered this for a moment. "I'll go with you," he offered.

"No. You have a firm, a very good firm. A firm firm." It was an old joke they shared.

"I'll take leave and…"

"You can help me move and even stay awhile, but you can't live there. We pushed you out of the nest, and now it's time for me to leave the nest too. And isn't the law firm starting to land some big fish, my efficient and reliable son?"

"I'll take the bar in Florida. Represent trophy wives in inheritance squabbles."

She opened the dishwasher and began to place silverware in its drawer, the stainless clinking as she dropped each into its proper slot. *Spoons… Forks…. Knives…* Order was soothing.

"Mom!"

"Everything in its place. Marry a jolly fat woman and come visit with a child under each arm. When I've had enough togetherness, crying and baby poop, I'll send you back up here and miss you terribly." She kissed his cheek then began to rinse the cups and put them away.

He looked at her, studied her as if he were deciding whether to take her case, or if he should ask the court to declare her insane. "I'm sorry," he said softly, and there was a little pause and a little sigh as though the last bit of air had escaped his body. "I'm sorry Dad died."

Sandy stopped what she was doing and looked at her lawyer son. She nodded. "Somehow," she said, "it all goes on. I didn't believe that at first." She finished putting the creamer away. "But I don't think I'm done yet, Robert. My marriage is over but *I'm* not over. Not yet. I'm still here. I'm still me…whatever that means. I just need to do something…different. Make a clean break."

Robert nodded and they hugged, and she saw how he tried to hide his eyes from her; and then he'd gone off to his apartment in Concord because he had a big case the next day *and a life of his own.* She went to her room and started to pack.

She thought of all this over the last sips of sherry, after which, Sandy walked home from the bar, undressed carefully, changed into her old shorts and t-shirt, and sat on her porch to watch the evening sky. The sun was setting behind Piney Point and splashed the underbelly of the clouds until the world burned red. As the water darkened and the sky cooled to purple, she saw - or thought she saw - a figure out on the sand spit. The wind had brought in the tide, and the figure seemed to be standing in shallow water. This was the way it happened before. . . a lone figure out in the water. Her chest tightened. She looked away, then back again.

"Edd . . .?" She squinted, but the figure seemed to have long hair and couldn't be Edd. Then, because the light had failed, had faded to make things formless and flowing, she saw nothing, only the imaginings of a lonely woman. Still, it gave her a sort of comfort, as though she were being tucked in for the night or pulling on a coat on a chilly morning. This surprised her.

The first time she'd seen it after her return to the island (after the business of the funeral and the move and the settling into the new house) as she sat on the Big Dock one evening. She had noticed a school of fish feeding and splashing out in the channel, only there was a human form there too; and like all those years ago when she'd visited with Edd, it was looking right at her. Thinking someone might be in trouble, she ran to the end of the pier and to see nothing, only wave shadows and seaweed. After that, she habitually searched the chop of waves or the sawgrass along the shore, peering into the wake of a porpoise, staring at a crab trap float, just to make sure something wasn't looking back at her and that all was as it should be.

Sandy began Sunday morning dressing for church, which, as it was neither Christmas nor Easter, was not a dress-up occasion; yet she wanted to look neither casual nor formal. *Like getting ready for a date*, she thought. It had been a long time since she'd actually dressed with a man in mind and she wasn't sure how to go about it. In the end, she chose black slacks and a loose white blouse because it seemed to hide her belly. She chose a shade of lipstick one shade brighter than she usually wore and made sure to apply it to both lips.

What do you think? She asked the mirror. *What would Edd think*? *He would probably say she was painting an old barn – Ha-ha!* She gave her reflection in the mirror a sad smile as she put on her pearl earrings.

It was an early fall morning with the sun still low enough to cast soft shadows as she walked, and her boldness grew as she went down the little hill to the white clapboard church. The business part of town sat beyond, Sunday sleepy and patient in the autumn air. She wondered if they used the word *autumn* in the south. A mockingbird alighted in a palm across from the church and began its morning practice.

According to habit, she arrived early and took her accustomed seat in the third row. There were only a few worshippers this early, and Pastor Helms was gliding from one to the other, shaking hands and making obligatory small talk.

He made his way down an empty pew and stopped before her. "How are you, Miss Sandy?" he asked, smiling his sideways smile, as though something were pushing against his jaw. "Made up your mind yet about that teaching position?"

A few weeks ago the Pastor had approached her about the need for Sunday School teachers, and she'd begged off by telling him that she was still moving in and needed to get settled. She'd felt guilty (which is what Edd said church was for). Today, she smiled up at him and said, "Perhaps during the winter months." And he nodded and shook her hand and walked away to greet someone else. She really did mean to volunteer, though she wasn't sure teaching Sunday School was her forte. Perhaps she could help organize a bake sale or a clean-up project. She knew nothing about children anymore.

Then she turned around and there was Bobby, as she'd hoped, sitting where he always sat, two rows behind her and off to the side, scrubbed and handsome. And there beside him sat *a woman* – a fly in her ointment. This was not part of the plan. If someone had been near Sandy they would have heard her inhale sharply, as one does in one's sleep. She turned around quickly, took the hymnal from the rack in front of her and studied it intently.

She'd recognized at once that the woman was sitting *with* Bobby, because she sat with the proprietary air women naturally recognize, a familiarity meant to show possession. For three months, Bobby Smeltzer had sat by himself, and on the one Sunday she'd made up her mind to invite him to do something he was sitting with a woman like they were…a *couple*. The verb form of the word flashed through her mind and she felt guilty for thinking such thoughts in church.

The introductory hymn began, tinkling notes scattering over the congregants like rain. Pastor Helms sang loudly in an effort to warm up the service. No one would know that Sandy was a mess. She stood and sat as directed and appeared to participate, even moving her lips during the singing, but no sound came forth. She heard none of Pastor Helms' sermon - something about Potiphar's wife - hearing instead an internal dialogue that accused her of being an old fool.

An angry fool, she thought, almost dropping the offering plate. *Why didn't I pay attention to him sooner, show him a little attention*? She laid her bulletin on the pew and pretended to brush something off her shoulder, glancing back to see the woman, who was looking back at her. The woman smiled and nodded with, Sandy thought, a shade of challenge behind her overly painted blue eyes. Bobby looked straight ahead and appeared to be listening to the sermon. After the benediction, Sandy slipped out the side door and walked briskly home.

The tide receded that evening. The sky was marbled with darkening pink clouds, and a small flock of birds scavenged along the spit, dashing ahead and away from her as she walked, stepping over conch eggs (*broken necklaces,* she thought), pieces of shells and ubiquitous sand dollars, waves lapping as the water withdrew to follow the moon. She saw something far out on the spit, but as she stared it turned into…what? A piece of driftwood?

Her house felt cold and dark and she slumped into bed early.

The following afternoon she ran into a woman - *Bobby's new woman* as she'd come to think of her - in the Zippy store. There were only a few aisles, which made it impossible to hide, and it embarrassed Sandy that she should even think of avoiding the woman, as though she were a rival, even though there was nothing between her and Bobby, and what the woman did was her own business. Well, almost her business. What one did in Cedar Key was everyone's business; such is the way of island towns.

Sandy had hardly moved in when the flotsam of gossip began to wash her way. There were the usual widows, like Miss Poteet, who made everyone's business their business, and there was a Women's Club that she didn't care to join; Sandy was convinced they existed only for the purpose of gossip. Miss Poteet kept her informed well enough. Still, she suspected there was something about an island, about being surrounded by the muddy Gulf, that provoked chatter and speculation disguised as friendliness, sharp and barbed as a ray's stinger.

"So nice to see you in church," she said to the woman when she found the meeting inevitable in the little store. It comforted her to see that without makeup, the woman appeared plain, even a little tired. *A few miles on her*, Edd would have said. Just so, the woman did not appear to have even the beginning of gills.

"Yes. Bobby's been after me to go forever and I just kept putting him off." The woman smiled. "I'm Mary Ellen," she said, extending her hand. "I tell you, after working all week I'm just worn out by Sunday morning. You wouldn't think art would wear on you, but it does. Saturdays have just been crazy." Miss Poteet had mentioned that a woman, an artist, had moved out to Hudson Hill recently. She'd said something about the woman making free-form sculptures out of driftwood, which Sandy thought was silly because driftwood had already been sculpted by wind and wave.

"I'm Sandy Collins," Sandy said, taking the woman's hand and feeling for a ring. There was a brief pause and both women smiled, as women do and then, "Well, I'll see you later, Mary Ellen." Then she went to study the lunchmeat in the refrigerated section.

That evening, Sandy called Robert. She liked to picture their voices bouncing along the miles of telephone line between Cedar Key and Concord, little atoms that flew back and forth like BBs in a garden hose.

"Hello, Son…and yes, everything is fine." She never called him on Mondays and didn't want him to think something was wrong. Of course nothing was wrong.

"Hey. Just walked in." She heard a female voice in the background, then his voice further away from the receiver.

"I can call later, Robert, if this…?"

"No. No. Cheryl was talking to me from the kitchen and didn't know I was on the phone."

"Cheryl?"

"You haven't met her, Mom. She works in the Public Defender's office, and we are going to fix whatever we can find for dinner."

This is I she get for moving away, Sandy thought. She wanted to talk, to be a part of his life, but it was too late. She was not there, and he was living his life. What else did she expect him to do?

"You okay?" he asked. She heard music in the background. The Doors played *Light My Fire*, though she didn't know that was the name of the song.

"I said I'm fine, dear. Just wanted to say 'Hello.' Listen…you've got company. Why don't I call you this weekend and we'll chat then?"

"You're sure you're all right, Mom?"

"Just fine, Son. Give my love to…?"

"Cheryl."

"Cheryl. And remember, a fat one with a baby under each arm."

"Funny. Goodnight, Mom."

"Goodnight, Robert."

Hanging up the phone can be a sad thing, she thought.

Sandy busied herself during the week by cleaning and washing things that were clean and washed, trying to forget that she was upset over something that didn't even exist, that she was behaving like a silly teenager. A dormant part of her had awakened, and she had no idea how to deal with it. She went for long walks out to the airport and to the ancient cemetery to wander among the clamshell-covered graves. She went to the little state museum but refused to walk past the woman artist's house on Hudson Hill. She walked around the big dock and watched the gulls scavenge tidbits from the fishermen and tourists. She spoke to no one, as Miss Poteet had gone to visit her sister in Atlanta, only exchanging polite pleasantries when she bought her groceries or slipped her mail out of the box at the post office. She still watched for Bobby, but the weather had been rough for a week and she only saw him go out a few times. Robert had begun to call frequently, and she knew he was worried about her, because it was the topic of every conversation, though she did her best to act cheerful and project a carefree attitude whenever he called. He insisted she come visit him or he was going to come down and visit her. She protested that she was fine and was still adjusting to island life. *Which was true*, she said aloud, startled by her own voice.

She began to attend church less and less.

In any case, busyness could only take her so far and that's when it happened. One chilly Friday night she found herself in the Poseidon Lounge listening to Guitar Joe sing about *Margaritaville* for the fifth time and she ordered a *second* sherry, which to most meant absolutely nothing, but to Sandy, was a crossing of the border, a finger pulled from the dyke, a spin of the cylinder, as significant as a dieter having that second slice of pie, or a smoker deciding to smoke just one after a decade of abstinence. She knew, though she would not admit, the second sherry would send her on her way. As she sipped, she focused on the painting behind the bar. Poseidon still had his arm around the redheaded mermaid while the blonde mermaid poured him a drink. Sandy thought she might dye her hair red. It seemed grossly unfair to her that Poseidon had legs, while the mermaids had to make do with scales and a flapping tail.

What could ol' Poseidon do with them, she thought, *they don't have the necessary parts!* A rosy glow seemed to emanate from the painting, filling her with warmth and sadness.

She ordered another sherry.

After a while, when the clock had spun toward closing, she walked a little unsteadily to Guitar Joe and asked him if he knew the song *Louie, Louie.* She asked, because she knew from her youth that the song only had three chords. He said he didn't but would try to learn it since he didn't get many requests.

"Ceee…Efffff…and Geeee," she said, mouthing each word slowly as if Joe were deaf and it might help him remember the progression. Then she turned, snapped a salute to Little Pete mopping up behind the bar, and went out the door. She did not see him look at the painting behind the bar and nod his head.

She decided to walk along the beach on the way home, rather than taking the road up 2nd Street. Although it was chilly, she leaned against a beached skiff and pulled her shoes off, enjoying the coolness of the sand as it molded to her feet. She saw that the tide was low, but the offshore breeze was quickening, and she knew from her tide chart that it would soon turn. She walked toward the spit, fiddler crabs making way, the males waving their one huge claw. In the moonlight, lines of seaweed from the last high tide ran before her as if to guide her down the beach. The breeze smelled like sad and long-ago music, and she pulled her windbreaker tight. Though it was dark except for the moon, she made out a few shapes (dolphins?) gamboling in the channel, and she envied them, their uncluttered lives and their freedom.

She looked over the water, and knew it was there waiting for her, out off the spit. She left the beach and traipsed over the mud, leaning into the wind now, and did not notice fingers of lightning probing the clouds behind Piney Point.

There! She saw it! Something in the water out as far out as you could go, at the very end of the spit!

Stay there, she willed the figure. *I'm coming to you. Just a little closer.* Then the squall came over the point and brought stinging darts of rain that made tiny clapping sounds on the waves. She walked in water, not caring that the tide had turned and, quickened by the wind now, would rush in to blanket the spit for the night. Between the crescent of the moon and the lightning flashes, she thought she could just make out, she stumbled over something in the water, a clump of shell or a piece of wood, as a sharp pain stabbed through her foot. She fell forward, throwing her hands out, going under in the undulating water, waves flooding her eyes with salt. Burying her.

Though the water was dark and cold, and the unknown lay around her, she felt surprisingly at peace; and though it may have been the sherry, it came to her how silly she'd been, concocting fantasies in place of acceptance and reality. Oh, how she'd missed the warmth of alcohol, the sense of certainty that comes with the soothing liquid, false though it might be. Something Little Pete had said came to her at the very moment she was…was what? Drowning? She thought she might stand; surely the angry water was, maybe, only chest deep.

Besides, she thought, *I have gills.*

"That that is, is," Little Pete had told her. Shakespeare or something. She wanted to stay on the bottom and sit like a stone in the lap of the muddy Gulf until she could sit no longer, and then…sit some more. She considered her circumstances, and though her lungs now burned in her chest and the cold did its numbing work on her body, she decided that, yes, that is exactly what she would do. She would sit and roll with the gelid tide until the very end. And then she would be with Edd again, where she belonged. She had been a fool to think she could start over. You could cover a scar with makeup, but it would always be a scar.

Bolts from the squall (on top of her now) began to arc across the black sky like tridents. Something swam by in a flash of blue light, as though it had a light of its own, or was lit from within. She'd read that sharks fed at night and that's why one should never swim then, much less sit on the briny bottom. *Mustn't sit on your briny bottom!*

She closed her burning eyes and when she opened them she was staring into the lightning-lit face of a…of a *female*…of a woman, long hair waving in the water, breasts no bigger than oranges. She felt a sharp tug and pain shot through her ears, then something – hands? -- pushed her. She kicked out and could not find the bottom and felt herself being lifted toward the rising and falling light. Her face broke the water and she gulped a huge breath before a wave slapped her hard, forcing black water up her nose, as the world narrowed down to a simple, airless nothing.

Shivering.

Cold.

Teeth clicking. Her left foot was on fire. From somewhere came the throb of a diesel engine. A blanket around her. A man held a light and peered into her face. Bobby. He was soaked. Had he been out on the spit too?

"You picked a heck of a time for a swim, Sandy! Most folks don't swim in the channel at night during a squall."

"Bobby…?"

"I was trying to beat the storm in and heard - saw, really - a lot of commotion. Figured it was porpoise feeding. Shone my light and there you were, bobbing like a crab trap buoy and covered in seaweed. What in the world? You looked like a mermaid."

"We're almost in," called a female voice. "How's she doing?"

He shone the flashlight into her face again.

"She'll live, Mary Ellen."

"Mary Ellen…"

"You know my cousin, Mary Ellen? She said you met in the Zippy store. Sometimes she goes out with me. Steers us in while I clean the boat. Keeps her off the streets." A pretend laugh came from the cabin. "This squall kind of snuck up on us."

Sandy grimaced, tried to sit up and touch her bleeding foot.

His cousin?

"You lost some skin there," Bobby said, straightening her leg. "Looks like you decided to kick some barnacles or oysters or something."

Then, warmed by the blanket and the mumbled voices of Bobby and Mary Ellen and the rhythmic throb of the diesel, Sandy closed her eyes and thought she dreamt as the boat rocked and made its way through the storm to the island. Finally the engine died, and she felt herself lifted onto a bouncing skiff which Bobby poled straight onto the beach. Then he carried her to her house, as Mary Ellen followed in the swirling rain.

As Bobby laid her in her bed, she wondered if he could smell the alcohol on her breath. But if he did he said nothing. Mary Ellen went to make tea. Bobby picked some seaweed out of her hair and when he pulled her hair back his eyes widened. He touched her ear lobes and said, "You are a woman of mystery, Sandy Collins." He held up his index fingers and she saw that they were spotted with blood.

"My pearls!" she cried.

She felt her earlobes and found them empty, bleeding where the posts had been ripped from the flesh. Yet her ears did not hurt.

Bobby looked at her closely. "The Gulf took your pearls," he said. "We'll get you some more."

They paused as they looked at each other and listened to the rain tattooing the tin roof. He laid his hand over hers.

"No," she said softly. "No more pearls." She thought she heard a splash somewhere far away, as though something large had entered the water and disappeared. Bobby frowned and shook his head as though he heard it too. "Gone forever," she whispered.

"You sure you're okay? I could run you to the hospital in Gainesville? It'd be no trouble."

She breathed deeply and liked the way Bobby's hand felt on hers. Strong and tender. She was, she knew, just fine. No, she wasn't just fine, not yet, but she knew she would be.

She placed her other hand over Bobby's and smiled and he quickly looked away.

Mary Ellen entered with the steaming tea.

And outside, the tide began to turn.

The Flight of the Eye

Sheri Hawthorne Carbone

Everyone in this world is granted special gifts and hidden talents, though sadly, most of us will never realize or recognize them.

This was not the case for Symwah, a young woman who longed to rise above her past and her surroundings.

Symwah had a dream each night that she could fly. And she discovered early in life that if she looked straight into the eyes of her beholders, and concentrated real hard, she could read their minds.

She was a quiet and gentle young lady raised in an orphanage nestled among the endless cornfields of Nebraska. Her parents had been killed in a horrific car accident when she was just a toddler, and her only surviving relative, her grandmother on her mother's side, who was already in poor health, found she could not raise Symwah without being tortured by the memory of the child she had lost.

Her grandmother sent the child to an orphanage at the age of three to be raised by a pair of sisters named Basa and Enda. The people of Nebraska called them the 'Sisters of Tomorrow,' and that is also what they named the orphanage.

The Sisters of Tomorrow orphanage was actually a small cottage in the country town of Beatrice, Nebraska, a place that was very hot in the summer and bitterly cold in the winter. The two sisters worked hard to find homes for each of the children that were brought to their orphanage, often without success.

Yet no prospective parent claimed Symwah. She was not one of the fortunate children.

Growing up in the Sisters of Tomorrow orphanage made the child feel unwanted, so from the time she was five, she grew increasingly shy and began to talk less and less, shrinking into corners and hiding in shadows. Instead of being the center of attention, Symwah gained an interesting vantage point to observe others.

The fortunate children came and went in the orphanage, finding homes, finding families, finding a place to belong. Through it all, Symwah clung to the corners like a ghost.

Yet, she did have one good friend. Her name was Bertha. She was born in Lincoln, Nebraska, and like Symwah, she was brought to the Sisters of Tomorrow at the age of three after her alcoholic and addicted parents were sent away to prison for drug trafficking. She was simply another child abandoned by fate and the poor choices of others.

Symwah and Bertha shared the same birthday, the same fears and the same dreams of life beyond orphanage walls and the vast, numbing cornfields of Nebraska. And on this, a friendship was born.

On their thirteenth birthday, Symwah and Bertha were given a birthday party by the Sisters of Tomorrow. There were balloons, snacks and a small cake with both their names on it, and for one day at least, they laughed and giggled with the other remaining orphans.

After the party, Symwah and Bertha sprawled across their beds and talked about what they intended to do once they turned eighteen and were forced to leave the Sisters of Tomorrow.

Symwah confessed that she always wanted to be a pilot. She had watched from her window as planes flew overhead and was carried away by the hum of their engines. To a young girl in an orphanage, the engines whispered songs of freedom and possibilities.

Bertha's dreams were more down to earth. She planned to be a nurse, because she imagined she might have been able to fix her mom and dad when they got into trouble with drugs. She knew it was too late to save her parents, but Betha's heart was open to helping others. It was after midnight when the two young friends slipped off to sleep, visions of the future still swimming in their imagination.

Symwah dreamed she was being chased again. It was the same terrifying nightmares that had haunted her ever since the accident that claimed her parents. A tall man in a dark coat was after her. She ran as hard as she could, but her legs were heavy and her steps were sluggish, as if she was trying to run through deep water. Then he was so close behind her, she could almost feel his cold breath on her neck. He reached out to grab her with two gnarled and filthy hands, when suddenly, she knew exactly what she had to do. She took a deep breath of concentration, bent her knees and launched straight into the sky! In her dream, she soared high in the air, where for once, she felt free, she felt safe and, and no one could hurt her.

When she woke the next morning, she found a single white feather resting on her pillow, and she knew it was more than a dream. She had flown! She was sure of it!

Symwah ran and giggled her way down the hall, practically leaping into her chair at the breakfast table. She knew that she couldn't tell anybody but her best friend that she could really fly. But while sitting in front of Bertha, she discovered something else. She focused on Bertha's blue eyes, and was hit by an overpowering feeling, as a thin, crystalline voice whispered in her ear.

I wonder why Symwah is so excited?

It was Betha speaking, though her lips were not moving, and no sound was coming out of her. Symwah suddenly realized she could read her friend's mind! She knew exactly what Betha was thinking!

"What's the matter, Symwah?" Bertha asked, but Symwah knew what she was going to say before the words even came out of her mouth. "What's going on?" Bertha asked, with increasing concern.

"Uh, nothing..." Symwah mumbled.

"Tell me. You gotta tell me."

"You won't believe me."

"Try me."

Symwah took a deep, shaky breath, then whispered, "I can hear your mind..."

Even before Bertha got up and left the table, Symwah knew her friend did not believe her. She could also sense the heavy blanket of sorrow that weighed on her best friend's thoughts, a sadness she had always tried to keep hidden, and just sensing that pain hurt Symwah's heart as well.

She learned that reading minds was not always a good thing.

To shake off the feeling, Symwah left the room and slipped out the back door. As she was walking slowly, she heard a rustling in the grass. She turned to see a pair of glowing green eyes staring at her. It was a coyote, grey, scrawny, and dangerous. She could tell by its bared teeth and snapping jaws that it was hungry. Her heart began to race, and she broke into a panicked run. The coyote chased her, gradually gaining on her with its greater speed and loping stride. Symwah ran as fast as she could but heard its cruel snarls so close behind her. She could even sense its primitive thoughts:

Hunger...Food...Death...

Just as the coyote leaped at her heels, the frightened girl stopped, crouched and willed her body straight up into the air. The coyote's jaws snapped at empty air, as she looked down from her vantage point dozens of feet above it. She was flying! This wasn't a dream…she could really fly!

And her life would never be the same.

Once the hungry coyote disappeared back into the grass in search of easier prey, Symwah floated back down to the ground and felt safe. But she was stunned to know that her dreams were revealing a new energy that had entered her body.

After the day's experiences, Symwah kept quiet about her gift for two more years. Some gifts were simply too personal to share.

Symwah had another experience when she and Bertha went to town on the orphanage bus to shop for clothes in the city. They were in a store looking at dresses, when Symwah suddenly felt an eerie chill zipper up her spine. She turned to see a tall man with a dark coat and sunglasses. He stood about ten feet behind them but seemed to be shadowing their every movement. When they walked, he walked. When they stopped to look at a dress on the rack, he also stopped and pretended to find something of interest in the small women's clothing store. Bertha had yet to notice him, even as he crept closer and closer. He slowly took off his glasses and Symwah had her first chance to look deep into his eyes. They were dark blue and filled with menace, his mind churning with anger and dark intentions. Those same evil thoughts screamed their way into Symwah's mind, as she fell into the whirlpool of his eyes. There was danger here; she knew it in every part of her being. Suddenly, the man reached for something hidden in his pocket, something dangerous, and Symwah knew she had to act.

"Help! Somebody help us!" she hollered with all her strength; her eyes never leaving the man's in the dark coat's malevolent gaze.

The customers were alarmed, and Bertha turned to Symwah in surprise.

"What's wrong?!" she asked, seeing her friend's strange expression. As clerks and customers came running to help, the man in the dark coat jerked around on his toes and vanished out of the store.

"Symwah, what just happened?" Bertha asked, grabbing her trembling friend by the shoulders. But Symwah could only whisper, her mind trying to free itself of the man in the dark coat's evil thoughts.

"Let's get out of here, now!" she said with a thin, papery voice.

The girls didn't buy a thing. Bertha pulled her friend into a nearby coffee shop, as they waited for the bus to return to the orphanage.

They both sat there stunned and Symwah looked into Bertha's blue eyes and she could read every question in her head. Symwah had no choice but to reveal her newfound gifts to her best friend. At first Bertha didn't want to believe her, but she could feel that her friend's sincerity, and quickly answered question after question, even before Bertha had her chance to ask them. The flying part was even harder to accept. Yet in all the time she had known Symwah, she had never known her to lie. Sometimes we must listen to those we love with an open heart, instead of a cynical mind.

Bertha wanted to know why she hadn't told her of these gifts earlier. But Symwah felt drained, and no longer in the mood to explain things that she herself didn't understand. Both girls were silent as they headed for the bus and returned to the orphanage.

It was during another birthday party, four years later, when Symwah's life would take another dramatic turn. A surprise guest appeared. Her name was Mrs. Nealy and Bertha jumped up and hugged her with tears in her eyes. It was her grandmother, the elderly woman who had left Bertha in the orphanage so many years ago. Looking into the older woman's watery eyes, Symwah could read the troubled thoughts behind them. Bertha's parents were being released from prison, after receiving parole for their drug-related crimes, and Mrs. Nealy wanted to bring Bertha home to reunite her broken family.

While Betha was excited about the news, Symwah felt a sinking in her heart. She could see that this was a bad move but couldn't ask her friend to turn her back on her real family. Besides, the Sisters of Tomorrow were desperate to make room for younger children needing a place to live. Symwah realized she had to let her friend go.

Mrs. Nealy filled out the papers in the office and the girls went to Bertha's room to pack. Symwah could read Bertha's thoughts and see that her initial excitement had turned to sadness and fear. Sadness at losing her best friend, fear of going back to parents she hadn't seen since she was three-years-old. The two friends hugged and cried and promised to never forget each other.

And then she was gone.

Symwah was so lonely that she'd often fly over the fields and let the trees keep her secret. For almost a year, she kept to herself, speaking very little and not even caring to read the thoughts of the other orphans. Then one day, she received a letter from Bertha saying that she could come and stay with her and her family. Even though she was still a month shy of her birthday, the sisters agreed to let her go early, since they wanted to reunite the girls. After all, the orphanage could only house girls until they were eighteen, when they would be considered emancipated under Nebraska law.

Symwah was a little scared to leave the Sisters of Tomorrow and the home where she had spent most of her childhood, but the promise of a new life filled her with anticipation. She took a Greyhound bus to Lincoln, Nebraska and Bertha, who now had her driver's license, picked her up at the station.

Symwah was so excited to see her friend they both had gotten taller and grown out of the awkwardness of their early teens. They chatted excitedly on the drive, almost as if they had never been apart. Such is the miracle of friendship.

Bertha told Symwah that her mom had passed away from a heart condition shortly after she came to live with her grandmother. Between the drugs and the long prison sentence, she never really got to know her mother. To make matters worse, her father had been drinking heavily ever since her mother died, and at times, his drinking really scared Bertha. By the time they arrived at Bertha's grandmother's home, Symwah had her guard up.

Mrs. Nealy seemed happy to have Symwah there and showed her to the bedroom she and Bertha would be sharing. As the elderly woman shuffled out of the room, Symwah noticed how much difficulty Bertha's grandmother had walking. She was clearly in a lot of pain and was grateful to have two young women around to help with the chores.

Just as Symwah was unpacking her few belongings, both girls heard screaming from the other room. Symwah was a little afraid to go out to the hallway, so Bertha told her to shut the door and she would go see what was going on. It was her father on another violent rant. He was holding a half-empty bottle of whiskey, knocking over furniture and tearing pictures from the walls, as he often did when he was very drunk. After he shattered a framed picture of Bertha's mom, Mrs. Nealy screamed that he needed to get out or she'd call the police. Symwah cracked the door and looked out into the hall. She could see the father and noticed something familiar about him. He had on a dark coat and looked very much like the man who used to chase her in her dreams, so many years ago. That scared her even more.

Bertha saw Symwah peering out from the bedroom, so she went back in and tried to comfort her. Both girls sat on the bed, as Bertha tried to explain that her father was still having trouble with the bottle. After her father had slammed the front door on his way out, the house fell strangely silent. Bertha asked Symwah if she wanted to go and have a soda at a nearby coffee shop, but they were afraid to leave her grandmother by herself, in case her father decided to come back drunker and angrier. They could still hear his loud ranting as he stumbled out into the street.

Another chill ran up Symwah's spine and she knew something bad was about to happen. A heartbeat later, they heard a terrible crash from outside. The two girls ran out the door moments after the accident. Bertha's father had wandered drunkenly into the street and caused a truck to swerve and lose control, pinning him to a telephone pole. He was dead on the scene. Bertha and her grandmother ran out of the house screaming, but it was all too much for Symwah. She opened a window, left her clothes and flew out the window over the city skyline. Symwah knew that she shouldn't leave her friend, but she had seen far too much tragedy in her short life. She looked down at all the commotion and it all felt strange to her, as if the reality was more of a nightmare than her dreams had been.

With tears in her eyes, Bertha looked up and saw Symwah flying away, framed by sunlight and clouds. Even in the midst of her anguish, the image gave her hope that someday, somehow, the world would offer an escape from the pain, and that she would see her best friend again.

With no explanation of how she was able to get back, the Sisters of Tomorrow welcomed the heartbroken Symwah back to the orphanage. They didn't need the ability to read minds to know the pain she was feeling. Even though she would age out soon, they told her she could stay another few months if she would help with the younger arrivals. Her old room was already taken, but they gave her a smaller one at the end of a hallway, with a window that faced the cornfield. Although they didn't know about Symwah's gift of flight, they saw how open spaces seemed to set her free.

After a few months, Symwah reached out to Bertha to apologize for leaving at such a crucial time of her life. She was surprised how quickly Bertha had forgiven her. In truth, seeing Symwah fly, and the secrets that only they had shared, brought the two young women even closer together. When Mrs. Nealy's increasing dementia and growing physical needs required her to be placed in a nursing home, Bertha again invited Symwah to come live with her. Her grandmother had put Bertha's name on the deed shortly after the young girl moved in to take care of her, and now the two girls would have a place they truly belonged.

As the years flew by, both women went on to discover their careers. Bertha became a nurse and helped people, young and old, find comfort amid their afflictions. Symwah pursued a career as a pilot and learned to fly in a different way. She found she no longer needed to read people's minds, as long as she just took the time to actually listen to what they had to say.

And that is how her heart really took flight.

The House With Two Front Doors

Lucy Mills

Friday

25th January 2018

Agnes Ellis' Diary

My journey was pretty routine. I bought my train tickets from the machine, got a coffee to go and took my seat in the quietest carriage. I travelled from city to countryside, from grey to blue, from glass to trees. It feels like London was keeping my troubles for my return, so I could enjoy this weekend away.

By the time I got to Rye the sun was beginning to set. The walk through cobblestoned streets was blissful. The only noise was from the seagulls and the pubs I passed along the way. I walked the sloping streets where homes loomed at obscure angles, casting long shadows. Trees and ivy latched onto homes, creeping up to the orange-stained sky. That's when I spotted the house I am now writing this in; The House With Two Front Doors.

True to its name, the house actually does have two front doors. Ivory bricks with coal-framed windows and two dark, shining doors in the center. The left door has the words 'The House With' engraved over the top, and the right one has 'Two Front Doors,' just in case anyone was unsure. Both doors have a letterbox, doorknobs, a lock and strange knockers, which look like a reaching arm reaching out with three pointed fingers. The devil coming for me, perhaps.

I chose the left door to enter.

The house itself is 'country chic,' as city folk might call it; white-paneled doors, with black beams lining the ceiling, and everything that can possibly have small floral prints on it, does.

I stood for a while and listened to nothing but silence.

Beautifully quiet.

That's all I want and that's all I've got, at least until my stomach started to rumble.

Transcript of video footage

The Mermaid's Inn

25-01-2018 19:27

A young woman enters the pub, looks around and walks towards an empty table at the back. She removes her coat and grabs a menu. She sits for a while, then walks to the bar and gives her order to the barman.

The barman leaves, then returns with a wine glass and a bottle of white wine. She takes them but stops as the barman asks her something. He raises his hand to indicate the number two. She nods to his question and there's an uncomfortable pause. It looks like he says sorry to her as he walks away.

The woman returns to her table. She is shivering, and her breath is visible. Everyone else in the pub is laughing and appears to be comfortable. The woman puts on her coat, rubs her hands together and looks to the blazing fire.

Transcription of video footage

The House With Two Front Doors

25-01-2018 23:11

A young woman enters through the right door. She stumbles, then shuts the door behind her, locking it. She flicks a switch and a dim overhead light comes on.

The woman takes her coat and boots off, staggering a bit as she does so, before she sits down on the sofa. She looks at the other front door and rummages in her coat pocket for her keys. She moves to the left front door and locks it. She walks back to her coat and stares straight into the camera mounted high on the wall.
She walks into the kitchen and sees another camera and stares up into it. She turns to leave, when she hears a knock on the door.

The woman goes to her coat to fetch the key when another knock comes from the right door. She grabs her keys and unlocks each door, even as more knocks are heard. She opens each door, but no one is there. Both door knocker are swinging, and she reaches up to stops them. Footsteps begin to echo from the floor above, and the woman looks up. She shuts both doors, turns to look up at the ceiling for the source of the footsteps.

She slowly ascends to the top of the stairs, stops and looks down at the floor. A track of muddy footprints lead to the master bedroom. She pulls out her phone, sighs and puts it away. She adjusts the keys between her fingers and approaches the bedroom door. She throws open the door and looks around. No one is there. She turns back to the landing and notices the footprints are no longer there.

The letterbox downstairs bangs open and closed, and she rushes back downstairs. The woman runs to the door and picks up an envelope. She opens the door, sticks her head out, then comes back in, locking the door, and stares at the letter.

THE LETTER

THE HOUSE WITH THE BENCH OUTSIDE
RYE
EAST SUSSEX
TN13 6AA
FRIDAY 25TH JANUARY 2018

THE HOUSE WITH TWO FRONT DOORS
RYE
EAST SUSSEX
TN13 6AA

To the Lady who is visiting,

I am writing to welcome you to our lovely village of Rye. It is but a small historical fishing village, though one with so much charm.

Are you alone? Or expecting anyone? We are very welcoming here and hope you feel that everywhere you go.

My name is Valerie West, your neighbor for your stay. How long are you staying, by the way? My house is the one with the bench outside. Our homes are sisters in names.

I just wanted to make sure you are feeling at home but thought it might be too late for me to pop round.

Feel free to write back. If not, I'll come around tomorrow evening to make sure you're all hunky-dory.

Yours truly,
Val

P.S. Do not worry about the cameras. They are not on. The previous owners put them in. I am not sure why.

Saturday

26th January 2018

Agnes Ellis' Diary

Yesterday was odd. The chill in the pub, the footprints and the letter. There are logical answers to all of them, I'm sure. There was probably a draught where I was sitting in the pub. I was a bit tipsy last night, so I could have imagined things. Kids where probably playing 'knock down ginger,' and the welcome letter is probably just that, welcoming.

So why does my mind always seem to drift to other answers?

I need to get out of this house today. I'll explore, eat some cake, chat to the locals and it'll be nice. Everything I want from this break. And yet, my thoughts keep getting distracted by everything that's happened over the last few months. It's supposed to be a new year and a new start for me, yet things are already…so strange.

Transcript of video footage

The Museum of Witchcraft in Rye

26-01-2018 10:48

Statues of witches line the room. In the center is the help desk with a young man sitting, reading. A nervous looking woman enters the dark lobby. She walks up to him.

AGNES: Excuse me

JAMES: Yeah? Oh, hi. *(Puts his book down.)* How can I help you?

AGNES: I want to look around the museum. I guess, like the majority of people who come in here.

JAMES: Oh, you're not like the majority of people who come in here. My name is James. Nice to meet you. *(He sticks out his hand. The woman shakes it).*

AGNES: Agnes.

JAMES: It's your lucky day, Agnes. I can take you on a free tour of the museum.

(The man leaves the desk and goes through a dark archway. The woman follows.)

JAMES: Welcome to the Grove of Mystics. Every item you see here is a real artifact used by witches in the Seventeenth Century, or ended in their demise...Why are you laughing?

AGNES: Well, they weren't really witches, were they? Just women who men didn't want to have around anymore. Or those with...mental health issues.

JAMES: Is that so? What about this then?

(The man strides to a glass case in the corner. The woman follows.)

JAMES: This is the cauldron of a witch named Henrietta Duke. She murdered the Lord of Rye by making a spell, in this very cauldron. The spell was so powerful, it made him jump off his Manor's tower to his death.

AGNES: You can't expect me to believe that. A cauldron isn't proof. She probably just made soup in it.

JAMES: A skeptic, I see. Perhaps you should read this...

(The man indicates an open book. He exits, while she stays to read from it.)

Extract from William Anderson's **The Witches of History**

(London, 2010)

[...] One of the most notorious witches of the seventeenth century was Henrietta Duke, for her devilish plot to become the Mayoress of Rye and spread Witchcraft throughout the land.

Henrietta was born to John and Betty Duke, who later had a second child they named Charlotte. They were a poor family living by the harbour with the other fishing families. John was out at sea for the majority of Henrietta's life. Betty had a job in the kitchens of the manor house at the top of the hill owned by Lord Christopher Wells of Rye. Henrietta took care of her sister, as well as other children of poor families whilst their parents worked.

It is said that Henrietta Duke was an incredibly beautiful woman and earned the admiration of many men, including Lord Christopher. She went to work in the kitchens when she was sixteen-years-old, which is where Lord Christopher first saw her. They married soon after, but on the night of their wedding, Lord Christopher jumped from the highest tower of his Manor, dying instantly.

It is said that Henrietta wanted power, after seeing what poverty had done to her family and others. She wanted to make radical changes that Lord Christopher disapproved of. It was rumoured she brewed a spell in her cauldron that would compel him to jump from the tower. It has also been claimed that Lord Christopher was deeply depressed and had suicidal tendencies, but the authorities considered these little more than idle rumours.

Henrietta was soon arrested by the Witch Finder General. According to the laws of the day, she was to be dropped into the harbour with stones attached. If she floated, she would be proved a witch. If she drowned, she would be found innocent of witchcraft.

Despite the weight of the heavy stones tied to her body, Henrietta was able to float above the surface of the water, and therefore, was found guilty of witchcraft. The Witch Finder General then held her underwater until she eventually stopped breathing. Witnesses claimed her younger sister Charlotte screamed as the sentence was carried out.

With her daughter judged to be a witch and a murderer, Henrietta's mother lost her job in the kitchens, lost her house and was thrown out into the streets. Her father did not find out about Henrietta's death until four months later when he returned from fishing. Charlotte drowned herself in the harbour a month later, presumably from grief.

Transcript of video footage

The Museum of Witchcraft in Rye

26-01-2018 11:11

(The woman closes the book and approaches the man by in the dark lobby.)

AGNES: None of this makes any sense! Lord Christopher clearly committed suicide.

JAMES: Really? It sounds to me more like envy.

AGNES: What?

JAMES: She was envious of his power and clearly wanted it all for herself. It was a chance to spread her wickedness.

AGNES: Seriously?

JAMES: Why else would she kill her husband on his wedding night?

AGNES: I don't believe she did.

JAMES: Of course, you would say that. You're a woman. You'll side with that witch whatever she did.

AGNES: I'm siding with her because I know what it's like when men don't believe you!

JAMES: Well, we all saw the news report.

AGNES: What did you say?

JAMES: We all know about you. It was all over the news.

AGNES: Everyone knows?

JAMES: It's the talk of the village. And as far as I'm concerned, that Andrew seems like a nice guy.

AGNES: You're disgusting.

JAMES: So why are you here, really?

AGNES: I was exploring the village, but I'd rather be anywhere else.

JAMES: I know the truth about you. We all do.

(The man grabs the woman by the arm. He begins to pull her further into the darkened museum. She starts to scream.)

JAMES: Come to read about your sisters long ago?

AGNES: GET OFF ME!

(The woman struggles to get free, then kicks the man in the groin. He doubles over in pain and releases her. The woman dashes for the exit, then stops as she sees a framed picture on the wall of The House with Two Front Doors with a smiling family standing outside: a father, mother and two young girls. The woman hesitates, then exits quickly.)

Audio Recording

Agnes Ellis' Mobile Phone

26-01-2018 11:23

SFX Background: footsteps and heavy breathing

LAURA: Hey, sis. How's the holiday?

AGNES: *(with tears.)* Not... good

LAURA: Agnes what's happened? Where are you?

AGNES: I'm walking up to the house I'm staying in

LAURA: Okay, get inside

SFX Background: Rattling of keys and heavy breathing. A door opens and closes.

AGNES: Ok I'm in.

LAURA: Take a deep breath and tell me what happened.

AGNES: This place... It's weird.

LAURA: Weird, how?

AGNES: This guy accused me of being a witch and then grabbed me.

LAURA: Jesus Christ, Agnes! Are you ok? Did he hurt you?!

AGNES: No, but...

LAURA: But it felt way too familiar...

AGNES: I came here to get away from all that...and now it feels like I need to get away from here too!

LAURA: Calm down, he's probably the village nutcase, and it's only one instance. Just stay away from him. You need this break after everything with Andrew...

AGNES: I just can't let it go.

LAURA: You're going to have to. To be able to move forward.

AGNES: I know.

LAURA: You need to believe it. I know others didn't, but I do.

AGNES: *(After a pause.)* I've got to go, Laura.

LAURA: Please don't.

AGNES: *(Another pause.)* ...bye...

Transcription of video footage

The House With Two Front Doors

26-01-2018 12:14

The young woman – Agnes Ellis - sits on the living room sofa with her phone in her lap crying. In the distance, another faint cry can be heard. The sound of crying gets louder and louder. Agnes looks up, angry and strides out of the living room, leaving her phone behind.

She walks into the kitchen and grabs a large knife. She follows the sound upstairs with the knife in hand. At the top of the stairs she stops, sees the muddy footprints again leading to the bedroom. She stands outside the door and slowly opens it.

She steps into the bedroom and flicks the light switch, but the light does not come on. She looks around. No one is there. She sits at the dressing table and looks into the mirror and jumps. She turns around quickly but looks into the space confused. Agnes turns back to the dressing table as a ghostly figure in front of her and screams. Agnes falls backwards, still holding the knife, but nothing is there.

The sound of whimpering can be heard again. Agnes slowly turns to look her at the bay window behind her. On the bench by the window sits the crying woman, more substantial than her previous ghostly form. The crying woman wears clothes from centuries ago. She is wrinkled, ugly and dripping wet.

AGNES: *(Voice trembling,)* Are you Henrietta? *(No answer.)* Are you Henrietta Duke?

CRYING WOMAN: They didn't listen.

AGNES: I understand, Henrietta. Believe me, I do.

CRYING WOMAN: They didn't believe me.

(Agnes slowly drops the knife and carefully approaches the crying woman.)

AGNES: They were wrong.

CRYING WOMAN: It doesn't matter who is wrong or right. It only matters who they choose to believe.

AGNES: Henrietta, I can help.

CRYING WOMAN: Why do you keep calling me Henrietta?

AGNES: You were the girl they drowned for witchcraft. I saw the picture in the museum. The picture of you and your family standing outside this house.

CRYING WOMAN: Henrietta was not a witch; she was the nicest person in the world.

AGNES: But...if you're not Henrietta...who are you?

(The crying woman rises, towering over Agnes.)

CRYING WOMAN: I am the one who killed Lord Christopher! I am the one who betrayed my sister. Who made her float... *(With pain.)* But I am also the one who didn't get to her in time... Even with all my powers, I couldn't save her...

AGNES: Charlotte...?

CRYING WOMAN: Yes.

(Agnes turns as a creak is heard from the landing. Suddenly, an older woman runs into the room. She picks up the knife Agnes dropped, rushes forward and stabs Charlotte in the chest. In her substantial form, Charlotte screams with anger and pain. She extends her arms and Agnes flies across the room. The older woman with the knife is hurled through the air and crashes down onto the landing. Charlotte's voice booms out with unearthly power.)

CHARLOTTE: You tricked me!

AGNES: No! No, I didn't!

CHARLOTTE: They don't believe you either. Any of them! To them you are just a whore! A dirty little slut, making advances on everyone! You weren't the victim. You were the pursuer! But you'll be my victim now!

(The doors bang shut, as a deafening wind swirls through the room. The large mirror explodes in a shower of glass. Charlotte grabs a shard of glass that cuts her hand and blood spurts from it.)

(Video feed dissolves to white static and abruptly cuts off.)

Sunday 27th January 2018

Email to Laura_M_Little@gmail.com

From Agnes.Ellis@gmail.com

[…] I thought it was over, she was coming towards me with that sharp piece of glass in her hand. Your whole life doesn't flash before your eyes, like they say. It's more like the important people come to you. And suddenly, you were there with me. Thank goodness, because you always know what to say. So I said what you always say to me…

I believe you.

I believe you.

Charlotte stopped for a long moment, confused. Then she fell to her knees and wept, like she had to get it all out, all those centuries of pain, and tears were the only way. I don't know why, but I crawled over to her, cutting my legs on all that broken glass. I was bleeding badly but still I hugged her. I hugged her hard and cried with her. Cried for both of us. And when I pulled away, she was young again. She was young and…lighter, somehow. After that, she just…disappeared.

I guess Charlotte spent her life defending her sister, trying to prove everyone wrong, and finally someone listened. I mean, she wasn't the nicest person. There was no denying she was a witch and that she killed Lord Christopher to try and take over his estate. But at least she had a chance to tell her story. She finally had a chance to be believed.

I thought I was doing the right thing leaving the city after they found Andrew not guilty. I felt I needed to get away, but I was wrong. I should have stayed and been with you and cried with you and talked and cried some more.

I'm coming back home tonight. I'm coming to yours.

Thank you for always believing in me.

Love always,
Agnes xx

P.S. Val is fine. Just some bruises.

Transcript of Nightly News footage

31-10-2018 18:23

REPORTER: Thanks, Claire. I'm here with Valerie and James West, the managers and owners of The Museum of Witchcraft in Rye, who claim to have definitive proof that witches and ghosts do exist. Good evening to you both. Tell me, Valerie, when was it that you thought the House With Two Front Doors was haunted by the ghost of Charlotte Duke?

VALERIE: A couple of years after I bought the house, odd goings on started happening. Strange things. Inexplicable. So I set up video cameras in every room, and that's when I first saw her. Charlotte. But she wouldn't talk to me. In fact, she was getting so violent, I had to move next door until I could find the perfect... communicator.

REPORTER: And that was Agnes Ellis?

JAMES: Yeah. We saw her on the local news after she lost her court case. I'd never seen someone so desperate to be believed. We both knew she would be the perfect conduit for Charlotte's spirit.

REPORTER: Some might say it was unethical to trap Agnes in a situation like that... Especially since you said yourself that Charlotte was violent.

VALERIE: Is it not vital to human progress to fully understand the past? With this evidence, Henrietta Duke has found some semblance of justice, and her sister Charlotte can finally rest. We have proved two things that have been debated for centuries; the existence of witchcraft and of the afterlife.

REPORTER: You still have no concrete evidence of Charlotte actually being a witch.

VALERIE: Yes, yes, fine. But we have video and audio evidence that ghosts are real. And that means anything could be. Isn't that the benefit that overpowers the losses?

REPORTER: Are you describing Agnes as a loss?

VALERIE: Agnes is an incredibly lovely girl who was at the center of some terrible things. And it's our hope she found some healing in all this as well. It's because of you, Agnes, that any of this is possible. Thank you.

REPORTER: Well you heard it here first. Ghosts are real. If you want to see the proof for yourself, everything will be on display in The Museum of Witchcraft in Rye.

Newspaper Man

Malorie Drake

Emma Grace, college student, sat in her dorm room with her head pounding. She had been trying to study for her upcoming exams for the past hour, and as the time ticked by, it seemed as if her hope of getting that done anytime soon was fading.

Emma peered over the top of her notebook at her roommate's sister who was currently spinning in a chair. Every time she would spin, it created an ear piercing squeak that was impossible to ignore. It probably didn't help that Kayla, her roommate's sister, seemed unable to insert a single breath between the stream of words that flew from her mouth. It was like the girl didn't know what the word *silence* meant. Emma's roommate Chloe just nodded her head every now and then, not really adding to the one-sided conversation. Emma stared at the two girls in the room hoping they would notice her look of "quiet down or leave," but neither did. They just kept chatting and chatting. It was apparent that the sisters had a mutual understanding of "you talk, I'll listen." All Emma desired, at that time, was a quiet place to study for her upcoming exams, but that wish seemed far out of reach, as the squeaking, squealing words merged into a brain-melting swirl of chaos.

Emma eventually decided she had no choice but to leave in hope of finding another place better suited to her study habits. However, it seemed that luck wasn't on her side today. As she wandered from place to place around the campus, she was confronted by non-stop storms of sound. She sighed in frustration, struggling to find somewhere, anywhere, else to be until her roommate's sister brought her noise level and incessant chatter back home to Alabama.

On her way to her favorite coffee shop, Emma was passed by Greenfield Park. She stopped, suddenly realizing she had stumbled across the perfect place. No annoying music or babbling roommates. Plus, she always heard that fresh air was good for your brain while studying.

The bench she picked to sit on was far enough away from the playground that she didn't have to deal with screaming children, yet close enough to the little streams that whispered tranquility as they ran through the park. Emma could hear the calming waters echo in the wind. She happily pulled out her books and notes and began, once more, to study for her exams. But after a few minutes, she looked up from her notes at something that teased her curiosity.

A little boy, around eight, sat on a bench only a few yards away. The small child stared intensely, in one direction, hardly even blinking. His unwavering focus poked and prodded hers.

After watching the boy for a few moments more, she started to grow concerned and rose from her study spot to walk over to him.

"Are you alright?" she asked.

"I'm fine," he responded quickly, hardly even meeting Emma's eyes before returning to whatever he was staring at.

Well, he said he's fine, Emma thought, *so I guess it's really nothing I should worry about.* She nodded to the boy before returning to her park bench cluttered with folders overflowing with class notes. Still, her eyes couldn't seem to let him go.

"Just focus on what you're doing. I'm sure he's just playing some new game he made up," she mumbled under her breath.

She went back to studying, with the peaceful wind as her only friend. The silence didn't last very long. The young boy walked over and flopped himself down on the small corner of the bench not covered with her school papers.

"So, what are you doing?" the boy lightly sang the question while looking up at her with bright eyes.

She gave him a curious look, but soon shook it off, and turned back to the definition she was to memorize.

"Trying to study for my exam," Emma flatly stated in hopes the kid would catch the vibe that she wanted to be alone.

"Oh," he responded. A few moments passed while Emma flipped through her papers, trying to ignore how intently the boy watched her. "Want to know what I'm doing?" he asked with a grin.

Obviously, he didn't catch the hint.

Knowing that, at this rate, she wasn't going to get any studying done, she turned to the boy.

"Sure. Enlighten me," she sighed closing her folder onto her lap.

His eyes filled with delight, as he said, "You see there's this man over there on that park bench." The boy pointed to the man on a bench a few feet away. "He comes here every day and never does anything but read his newspaper. I've been watching him for weeks now, and he doesn't react to anything. Ever!"

Emma glanced towards the older gentleman reading his paper, with a pile of other newspapers stacked on the bench beside him. He seemed normal. There was nothing peculiar in ways of appearance.

A red Frisbee flew past the man's head, yet he remained like a statue, not even flinching. His eyes remained glued to the newspaper. The kids playing with the disk yelled an apology as they scurried away, clearly frightened by his stoic disposition.

"Ok, I'll admit, that's a little odd," Emma said after having observed the man's behavior.

"You're telling me," the boy laughed lightly. "I even tried talking to him a few times, and he acted like I wasn't even there." The boy dramatically paused as he whispered his last few words, "I'm starting to think he might be a ghost!"

"Maybe he just wants some quiet," she said with a sigh, once again hoping the boy would take the hint. But he just shook his head more forcefully.

"Nah, I don't think so. Why would someone come to the park for quiet when they would just be bothered by kids?"

Emma realized the boy was right about one thing. Coming to the park for peace was a bad idea after all. Emma put away her things as she spoke knowing that after whatever would happen next, she'd be better off finding a new location to study.

"Hey, you wanna make a bet?" he asked, his voice ringing with excitement.

"What kind of bet?"

The boy put his hands on his chin in deep thought, as he looked around the park that surrounded them.

"How about if you can get the newspaper man to respond to you. I'll buy you an ice cream. If you fail, you have to buy me one!" He wiggled in his seat like a dog wagging its tail.

"Uh, do you even have any money?" Emma asked. Even if he did, would she want to take money from a child?

"Yeah, I have some. I did extra chores around the house this week, so I have enough to buy one ice cream cone." The boy's face lit up as he spoke. "Don't worry. So is it a bet?"

"I don't know…," Emma hesitated, shoving the last of her papers into their bulging folders and books.

"Oh, c'mon! Please?! I'll be good on my word, I promise." The boy stared up at her with the biggest puppy dog eyes he could muster.

Great, she thought. *Taking ice cream from a child is no better than taking candy from a baby.* But Emma couldn't say no to such pitiful looking eyes. That was why her little sister got away with so much, before she went off to college.

"Okay, why not?" she sighed. "A little ice cream never caused any trouble." Emma stood and began making her way over to the old man and his morning paper.

"You can do it!" the boy yelled to her, adding a 'thumbs up' for good measure.

In the twenty or thirty feet it took to reach the old man's bench, Emma realized she had no idea how to start up a conversation with this complete stranger, and she felt even more embarrassed as she stood over him and his paper.

"Um, H-Hello," she choked out. "Nice weather we're having, isn't it?" But the man remained focused on his paper, as if he hadn't heard her, or seen her standing over him. His lack of reaction made her feel both silly and a little annoyed, but she was here, and the boy was watching them both and she had to continue with the bet.

"They say it's supposed to stay sunny almost all week. At least until the rains come on Saturday."

Still no response came. Actually, she didn't blame the man at all. This was the most boring conversation she'd ever heard. Well, other than that one time her friends argued spent an entire afternoon arguing whether chicken nuggets were better than chicken strips.

"You know," she said to the man and his paper. "I've been reading this book on helium and I haven't been able to put it down." It was a corny joke, and she grimaced as the words left her mouth. Still there was no response. Obviously, this guy didn't have the same sense of humor as her Science teacher. At least bad jokes were better than a mindless conversation about the weather. "Do you know why plants hate Math?" she tried again. "Because it gives them square roots." Emma moved her hands as if she were executing a drum roll on some cheesy comedy show.

The man never looked up from his paper or spared even a glance in her direction.

Apparently jokes are not his cup of tea, she thought, suddenly realizing she may lose this bet. *Guess I'll have to do something crazy instead. Something so weird he would have to pay me at least one ounce of attention.*

Emma had one last trick up her sleeve. She slowly bent her knees as she took a few steps forward, dropping her body as if she was walking down invisible stairs.

It was an old mime gag, but it had to work. It always made her little cousins giggle, and really, who could possibly ignore a girl acting like she was walking down a non-existent staircase in the middle of a public park?

The man huffed as he folded the corner of his newspaper down to glare at her. The look clearly told her he wanted to be left alone, and that she had better do just that. Then he buried his scowl back in his paper and pointedly ignored her. Taking that as her cue to leave, Emma skipped her way back over to the boy, who was obviously thrilled by her performance.

"Woah! You actually got him to look at you! You must be a wizard or something!" Then the smile faded, as realization hit the boy. "Oh, I guess that means I lost…"

There was so much disappointment in his widened eyes. Emma shook her head and plopped down on the bench beside him.

"I don't think one look really counts as a reaction," she said softly. "Especially a glare like that one." She didn't have to fake a shiver, because the glare was actually quite scary. The old man may not be a ghost, but he had looked at her with such annoyance in his eyes, she couldn't really claim it as a win. "That old man really gave me the heebie-jeebies," she whispered in her best ghost story voice. And as the boy laughed, she added, "Come on. I'll buy you an ice cream."

"But I didn't win?" The boy dropped his head in defeat.

"Take the ice cream or not. It's your call, kid." She sighed dramatically as she picked up her backpack, turned and pretended that she was really going to leave. "But you better hurry before I change my mind…"

"Wait for me!"

Emma grinned, as the boy leaped off the bench and ran to her.

"Come on. I'll race you to the ice cream vendor!" She laughed as the boy's eyes widened, and he took off towards the ice cream cart a short distance away.

After she bought them both ice cream sandwiches, Emma bid the boy a goodbye and continued her nearly hopeless journey to find a quiet place to study.

The boy shuffled back to the bench and watched as Emma walked away. When she was finally out of eyesight, he jumped up and skipped over to the newspaper man, smiling from ear to ear.

"It worked again, Grandpa!" he exclaimed.

The old man flipped down the corner of his newspaper.

"As expected," he winked at the boy, then carefully folded his newspaper and added it to the stack beside him.

The boy broke the ice cream sandwich in half, giving part of it to his Grandfather before climbing onto the bench next to him. He swung his little legs back and forth, as both nibbled their ice cream sandwiches in blissful peace.

"You know Grandpa, I've been thinking," the boy said after licking the last drops of ice cream off his fingertips.

"Now, that's dangerous," the man old man chuckled taking the last bite of his sandwich.

"Maybe we should start doing something bigger than ice cream sandwiches? Like maybe snow cones, or maybe even a Happy Meal!"

"You think we could pull it off?" he asked, seeing the mischievous glint in his grandson's eyes.

"Why, of course! You always tells me that the first step in getting what you want is remembering that you can't have *confidence* without a *con*." The boy smiled up at the old man.

"Your Grandpa sounds like a smart guy..." The man smiled back and fist-bumped the boy. "…with an even smarter accomplice!"

"No doubt about it," the boy giggled, as he imagined a future filled with snow cones and hamburgers.

Ulricke Klackenbach

Michael Noonan

"The question is when?" whispered David Morrison, hoping his nervousness didn't show.

"I strongly suggest next Friday," said Charles Deakin with a wry smile. "Friday the thirteenth, by the way. I hope you aren't superstitious about these things."

Morrison shook his head. "I guess that's as good a day as any."

"Most of the executives and the staff will be at the Grand Hotel. Celebrating the fifth anniversary of the founding of the company. It's going to be a swell party," Deakin continued, in full conspiracy mode. "Of course, Ms. Klackenbach won't be there. Because, as we all know well, she doesn't like parties. So things should be much quieter at the office."

There was a long pause as the two men considered the risks and implications of what they were planning to do.

"Okay, let's go for it then," said Morrison, with grim finality.

"I say we try and leave it as late in the office day as we can. Wait until the rest of the staff have left; and only we and Ms. Klackenbach are still on the premises. She always leaves an hour or more after everyone else has gone," said Deakin. "Then it's just a matter of getting into her office, and getting the job done."

"What about her secretary, Mrs. Fathom?"

"Hopefully, she will be gone too. If not, we will have to take care of her in a different way."

"Of course, when it's all over with, you and I will have some explaining to do," said Morrison, a grim smile pulling at his lips.

"It'll look bad at first," said Deakin. "There's no getting around that, Dave. But when they finally examine her body, and see what kind of creature she actually is, it'll put a whole new complexion on things. After all, you can only murder a human being."

The word 'murder' caused another wave of sweat to break out on Morrison's forehead.

"It's up to us, Dave. And you know it's the right thing to do."

"I know, but what if…?"

"Let's get the job done first. That's the crucial task. Then we can talk about the consequences."

Morrison nodded, and after making sure they hadn't been seen, the two men left the park in different directions.

It was Thursday the twelfth. The day before everything they had planned for months would become real. The day before all hell would break loose.

All that evening Morrison felt acutely nervous and ill-at-ease. His stomach ached and he tried hard to hide the shaking in his hands. He slaked dry cups of coffee, had a few stiff whiskeys, and even slipped outside on occasion to smoke cigarettes; recent events having driven him back on a habit he thought he'd seen the back of. When he was back inside the house, he could hardly keep still in his chair.

"Are you all right, David?" asked Janet. Her husband's pacing and uneasy presence made it hard for her to concentrate on her favorite soap opera.

"Yeah. Just got a slight fever, that's all." He hoped she would consider that a plausible excuse.

"Well, those cigarettes you've been sneaking out to smoke won't help."

"The pressure's been piling up in the office these last few weeks. I'm just using them to calm my nerves. When things get back to normal, I'll kick the habit again."

"You look all done in. You could do with an early night."

"Yes, you're probably right, Janet."

"And tomorrow I'll ring in and tell them you're too ill to go to the office."

Her words almost made him jump out of his chair. *Not tomorrow! Not after everything they had planned!*

"I'm afraid not, dear." He did his best to calm his voice, unable to meet his wife's eyes. "I've got to go in. Whatever I feel like. Even if they have to carry me in on a stretcher. I've a report to complete, for a high level executive meeting. It can't be delayed. And there'll be no advancement or promotion for me if I botch this one." He smiled uncertainly. "But I promise I'll report in sick the day after."

She shook her head. There was no arguing with him when it came to the office. "I hope you're doing the right thing," was all she said, before her attention drifted back to the television.

Another sleepless night left David Morrison even more frazzled than before. Slumped over the table, he half-heartedly crunched his way through a tasteless breakfast cereal, and barely tasted the coffee he downed in three gulps. In his blurry self-absorption, he failed to notice a black cat perched on top of the garden fence. The large feline seemed to glower at him with a strange intensity, peering through the open blinds of his kitchen window, as if mysteriously aware of the fears that assailed the uneasy conspirator. When

Morrison did finally glance up to the window, his eyes locked with the unfamiliar creature, before it suddenly leaped down from the fence and sped away.

"That's funny," he mumbled to himself, "I haven't seen that one before." He turned to his wife, wiping off the countertop. "Janet, do we have a large, black cat in the neighborhood?"

She considered the question for a while. "Not one that I'm aware of. Why?"

"I saw one staring at me just now. From the garden."

"It must be a stray."

"I daresay."

"You're not becoming superstitious, are you?" she asked with a grin.

"Y'know, you're the second person to ask me that question in the past few days."

"Well?"

"No more than the next guy, I suppose."

"I've never known things like that to bother you before. You've always been so damned practical. Anyway, black cats only bring bad luck if they cross your path."

"So they say."

She shook her head. "It's all nonsense, of course."

"Of course." He nodded, before relegating all thoughts of stray pets to the back of his mind, having far more serious matters to consider.

A short time later, David Morrison picked up his heavy briefcase, pecked his wife on the cheek, then left for the office. Janet watched from the upper window as he turned down the garden path. She frowned when she saw a large black cat bound from one side of the garden, and speed across the path just before him, before jumping over the fence and disappearing from sight.

Morrison turned back to his wife, framed by the window. They both raised their eyebrows and shrugged their shoulders, each pretending it was nothing more than silly superstition.

He left his vehicle in his reserved spot in the car park, then made his way into the reception area of the headquarters of Lifeblood Technology, Incorporated, his place of work for the last three years. An office environment that felt increasingly alien to him these days. He closed the door to his cramped office and snapped opened his briefcase. For the fifth time that morning, he checked to make sure the weapons he would need were still safely hidden under the stack of documents inside. He closed the briefcase and tried not to think about the grim task and gory scene that lay ahead.

He met Charles Deakin in the washroom at exactly 3:15 PM, as planned. They swapped strained small talk about the weather and a recent sports game, until a third work colleague finished washing his hands and left. Once they were sure they were alone, the two conspirators reviewed the final details of their plan, gravely wished each other good luck, and parted for their respective offices.

Ulricke Klackenbach was the founder and chief executive of Lifeblood Technology Incorporated. She was a slender woman, just shy of six-feet-tall, with jet-black hair, and a high-cheeked face of severe beauty. She had gleaming white teeth and always wore her trademark, blue-tinted spectacles. Ulricke Klackenbach was in her early forties and of Central European origin, though it was difficult to pinpoint exactly from which country by her odd accent and strange manner of speech. She was considered a strange, reclusive figure, who spent most of her time in her personal office, communicating with the rest of the staff only through phone, intercom or e-mail. Her private office was dreary by design, and seldom seen by most of her employees. The window blinds were never opened, and the sun's rays never penetrated the room. The only strong source of light was a halogen table lamp, with flexible stem, positioned on the edge of her large desk, that she would use to illuminate whatever documents she happened to be studying. Those few privileged staff members who were allowed to enter her office found it to be a distinctly grim and depressive place and were frequently all too glad to see the back of it. Indeed, a number of them had described it as feeling like they had been trapped in a cave. By contrast, the rest of the office was chic and smart, stylishly decorated, well-lit and welcoming of sunlight.

The justification for Ms. Klackenbach's cheerless, penumbral environment was severe migraine headaches, as well as an unusual sensitivity to light, which also explained her tinted spectacles.

Even outside the confines of the office there were whispers about her mysterious existence. She was single, seemed to have little or no social life, and never mixed with executives or staff outside of business hours. Indeed, only a handful of top company insiders had any idea where she lived. Ulricke Klackenbach was known to be tight-lipped and unforthcoming about her past. She was, as someone had once reflected, a riddle wrapped in an enigma. She stayed hidden in her private office, arrived and left the premises by a special corridor, to which all the rest of the staff were denied access. It was rumored to be directly connected via a door in the back wall, for which she alone had a key. She was taken to and from the building in a large, sleek limousine, with curtained windows. Though a fierce negotiator and thorough professional with an acute business sense, she appeared taciturn and self-contained to an almost morbid degree. That icy reserve and aloofness only served to sour and darken the atmosphere within the company, and most employees were grateful to have little or no contact with her.

Charles Deakin, an accountant, had joined the company three years earlier. David Morrison, a sales executive, arrived shortly after that. Both men were in their late thirties; both were jazz buffs and they supported the same football team. They shared other interests and enthusiasms, and as a result, struck up an immediate rapport and became close friends.

It was about that time that a series of inexplicable murders took place within the city. They were seemingly random killings, always at night, and in various quiet localities. The victims were of both sexes and ranged from teenager to pensioner. That had done much to spread panic throughout the city and kept many a citizen off the streets at night. When people did venture out, it was generally in the company of others, for mutual support and protection.

Only two things connected the killings; two puncture marks on each victim's throat, and the bodies were almost entirely drained of blood. Not surprisingly, the media referred to the elusive killer as 'The Vampire.' Despite an intensive police investigation, no clue had been unearthed as to the identity of the killer.

Then, three weeks ago, Morrison believed he had stumbled across what could be an explanation to that mystery, and it chilled him to the bone. As with many others in the company, Morrison had always felt there was something distinctly disconcerting about his female employer. Though he had never really suspected how far she differed from the general run of humanity until the day he was called into her office for a private meeting to discuss an issue concerning the sales department. It was the kind of minor problem she usually dealt with over the phone, so it was something of a mystery to Morrison why she had insisted on this face-to-face discussion in the first place. It was the first he had ever had with her, and what happened in that private meeting shook him to the core.

He was still trembling when he talked about it with Charles Deakin later that day.

"What first struck me as odd was that there was a full-length mirror hanging on the wall. I always thought she had a strange aversion to mirrors. Didn't like them anywhere near her. Indeed, someone once told me she didn't even carry one of those little compact mirrors that women carry to apply their make-up."

"Yes," Deakin agreed. "The only mirrors in the whole office are the ones in the washrooms."

"But you haven't heard the half of it yet."

"Go on."

"I looked into the mirror. And, as you'd expect there were reflections of the room, of objects in the room, and of me. The only thing without a reflection was our boss, Ms. Klackenbach!"

"Are you sure?!"

"Absolutely! Where she should have stood, there was no reflection. Only empty air. Though she pretended to be unaware that I had noticed it at all..."

"But that's…impossible!"

"I know. I looked into the mirror several times, just to make sure." He paused. Shuddered. "This woman casts no reflection. And what kind of creatures do they say neither casts reflections nor shadows?"

Both men fell into a troubling silence. As it dragged on for a painfully long time, Morrison began to worry his friend would think he's crazy.

"It explains a lot. doesn't it?" he continued with fierce sincerity. "That's why she's such a reclusive figure… Why she hides inside her office with the lights low and the blinds closed… Why she keeps the rest of the world at arm's length!"

Deakin's voice trembled as he spoke. 'Are you seriously telling me we've been working all this time for…what? A vampire?"

"I know it sounds insane, but it sure looks that way. Don't tell me you haven't felt it too?"

Deakin was again silent for a long time. When he looked up at last, his voice trembled, as he whispered, "But why here? Why now?"

"I don't know. Maybe their kind have always been among us. Feeding on us for centuries… Maybe this whole company just serves as some kind of a front. I suppose even vampires have to earn a living in this world. They can't all be Counts hiding away in Medieval castles. Not in the Twenty-First Century."

Deakin shook his head. 'But what I can't understand is why did she ask you to her office, then arrange for a mirror to be there? She must have known you'd be able to see it? See what she was… Why deliberately give herself away like that?"

"I don't know. Maybe it's her way of trying to get me to quit?"

"Did it make you feel like handing in your notice?"

"I'm still of two minds about it. How should you act in a situation like that? Run away with all those killings that have been happening lately? Or do we do something about it?"

Deakin nodded his head. 'If what you're saying is true, she could well be connected with the recent murders."

"Who else could commit such inhuman crimes? Let's face it, Charles, everything points to our boss being the murderous 'Vampire' terrorizing the city"

"But if the mirror is still hanging on the wall of her office, anyone who goes in will know she's a vampire..."

"It isn't there anymore."

"Huh?"

"She asked me back just an hours later, over another trivial matter that could have been dealt with on the phone. I was scared to go back, but I just had to see if I imagined the whole thing. But when I went into her private office again, the mirror was gone. And somehow I doubt it will ever be back again." He ran a trembling hand through his thinning hair. "It's as if she *wanted* me to know what she really is."

Over the days and weeks that followed, the two coworkers talked at great length about what they should do with their appalling discovery, though always outside the confines of the office. They did their best to talk each other out of the wild conclusion they had come to, but after a few more nighttime murders on the edge of the city, they decided, with icy misgivings, they had no choice but to act.

They seriously doubted that the police would take their claims about Ms. Klackenbach's culpability for those crimes with any seriousness at all. They would be called lunatics.

Or worse...

"We'd be laughed right out of the police station!" said Deakin, "And what would happen if our boss ever found out we had reported her to the police?"

Morrison shuddered. "We'd both be dead that very same night."

"Along with our families," Deakin added, his face ashen.

"Along with our families…"

With a vampire being a supernatural creature, they decided it was extremely doubtful the authorities, and their conventional police methods, would be of any use countering the evil power that such a being possessed.

"If we want to prevent more innocent victims from being hideously murdered, we have to take matters into our own hands."

Fortunately, both men had read enough vampire stories and seen enough horror movies to know how to deal with a creature like Ulricke Klackenbach. It would have to be a stake driven through her heart. By such grim means alone could one be certain of destroying such a loathsome creature who was terrorizing the city at night.

"She might look like a human being,' reflected Deakin, "but this is a monster who poses a deadly threat to all our lives! She must be eliminated. In the same way you'd destroy a plague or virus."

"And we alone are the antidote…," muttered Morrison.

To David Morrison the day of the evil deed dragged on like a small eternity. He drained cups of coffee from one of the offices vending machine and was forced to slope out of doors every so often, in order to sedate his nerves with cigarette smoke. Such was his fragile state that he wondered every few minutes whether he could even go through with the plan. A venture that the more skeptical side of his nature told him was a crazy idea to begin with!

The details had been carefully worked out. They would hope Mrs. Fulcrum, Ms. Klackenbach's secretary, would be gone for the day. She was the one who manned the desk outside Ms. Klackenbach's private office and carefully monitored who went in or out. If she didn't leave, they would render her unconscious with an ether-soaked handkerchief, then gag her and tie her to her chair. They would force open Ms. Klackenbach's door with an iron jimmy, and hopefully, take her by surprise and deal with her by the time-honored means they had already discussed.

At 5:30 that evening, they met in the men's washroom as planned.

Morrison, pale and trembling, looked like he was deathly ill as the time drew near. By contrast, Deakin seemed unusually calm, especially considering the grisly job they were about to undertake, and all the risks and uncertainties involved. Morrison envied his friend's previous experience in the military. Instead of going into battle with an undead creature, Deakin looked as if he was about to enter her office to ask about a pay rise.

"Yeah. They've all left now, Dave," he said. "We have the place entirely to ourselves. Apart from Mrs. Fulcrum, and you know who."

Morrison looked at his partner with open admiration, almost tinged with a certain amount of guilt and self-recrimination at his own all-too-human fears.

"You're taking this all in your stride, Charles, I must say. I've been sweating buckets and I can hardly keep my hands still."

"The key is to keep your mind focused and your attention on the job in hand. That's all there is to it."

Morrison shook his weary head. "Keep focused," he mouthed to himself. "I can hardly think straight these days."

"It's going to be over quite soon, Dave," Deakin assured him. "Sooner than you think."

In a few minutes, all being well, they were to incapacitate and tie up Mrs. Fulcrum, burst into Ms. Klackenbach's office, clasp hold of her, pull her across the polished surface of her desk and drive a stake through her living heart. And thereby

They walked out of the washroom and made their way to the anteroom to Ms. Klackenbach's office, determined to rid the city of the inhuman predator that had destroyed so many innocent lives.

It was indeed a tall order for a day at the office.

Morrison felt his heart pounding in his chest, and he felt himself slipping into some unreal and repellent nightmare.

They received their first piece of luck when Morrison noticed that there was no one in the anteroom.

"Mrs. Fulcrum isn't here," he whispered. "There's no one behind her desk!"

"Calm down, Dave. She's might just be in the ladies' room. But either way, it makes our job easier."

Morrison tried to bury his shaking fingers in his pocket. "D'you think we should be going through with this at all, Charles? I mean, what if we're wrong? What if we're making some ghastly mistake? I mean, we're talking about vampires and crucifixes and stakes through the heart here?! Maybe we should just call it off? Before it's too late."

"We can't back out now, Morrison," he said calmly. "The die has been cast."

And with that, Deakin moved to the window to look out over the darkening city. As he walked past a wall lamp, electric shudder of alarm coursed through Morrison's body and shredded what remained of his already tattered nerves.

There was no shadow.

Charles Deakin had no shadow.

And that was the moment a sudden wave of fear and nausea hit David Morrison. His mind reeled and he was forced to hold onto the wall to secure his unsteady legs.

After scrutinizing the first edge of darkness slip over the high-rises of the city, Deakin turned back and smiled at his distraught companion. *That was why he seemed so casual and unconcerned about the whole thing.* Morrison also noticed, for the first time, how pale and bloodless his friend seemed, with that eerie smile and glacial look in his eyes. And something Morrison had failed to notice before…just visible below his collar, two red puncture marks on Deakin's neck.

"Not long now," said Deakin, with chilling assurance, as he turned back to view the urban panorama over which the subtle shade of evening was gradually creeping.

Slowly, tentatively, Morrison edged back towards the corridor, and whatever safety it may yet hold. He had to leap back, as the door to the private office flung open and Ulricke Klackenbach entered, dressed from neck-to-toe in a shimmering black gown. In her arms she cradled a black cat. The very one that had glared at Morrison from his garden fence that morning. Its eyes were half closed and it purred contentedly as his boss' thin fingers stroked its silken fur.

Through the same door poured the rest of the executives and company staff, who were said to have attended a party at the Grand Hotel an hour ago, entered the anteroom. Each one stared at Morrison with a mixture of contempt, pity and…

…hunger?

Morrison, now in a blind panic, tried to turn and, but found his path blocked by his former colleagues. Colleagues who now seemed utterly alien to him.

"I hope you're not thinking of leaving us, Mr. Morrison," Ulricke Klackenbach said, as she gently placed the cat down on the carpeted floor, from where it critically scrutinized Morrison. "Why, the party's hardly begun."

"Why are these people here?" Morrison gulped hard. Why aren't they at the Grand Hotel?"

"But this is where the action is," smiled Ms. Klackenbach.

They all began to circle Morrison, their eyes red with hate.

"Get away from me, you…you vile abominations!"

"Now, now, Mr. Morrison," said Ms. Klackenbach. "There's no need for name-calling. These are your colleagues and coworkers. You must treat them with respect." She turned to two burly members of the security staff. "Grab hold of him, please," she instructed.

They clasped hold of Morrison, and despite his struggles, dragged him back into the middle of the anteroom.

Another worker from his own Sales department picked up Morrison's briefcase and handed it to Ms. Klackenbach. She opened it and pulled out a hammer, a sharpened wooden stake and the iron jemmy. With a shudder, she chose to leave the crucifix where it was.

"A regular handyman, isn't he?" The crowd laughed and crept closer, then she turned to Morrison. "I'm afraid you won't be needing these tonight, my friend." She dropped the vampire-killing tools to the carpet.

"How in hell did you find out about us?" Morrison said weakly.

"You could say a little creature told me."

The cat, one of Ulricke's most trusted familiars, bared its fangs and hissed at Morrison.

"You can't hide anything from me. I knew about your pathetic little conspiracy from the very beginning." She smiled with a strange serenity, as a cold blue light danced across over her moistened lips. "You thought you'd discovered my secret. But I deliberately left the mirror there, Mr. Morrison, so that you would notice one or two particularities about your employer."

"But why? Why the game?"

"You were becoming too inquisitive for my liking. I could see the suspicion in your eyes. And I could read the thoughts that you sought to hide. No one can keep secrets from me. It's a gift of my kind. A very useful one." She turned to Deakin, who looked away with… what? Shame? Then she turned and aimed her blue-tinted sunglasses back to Morrison. "In any case, I decided to bait a trap. And you obliged by walking right into it."

Morrison looked down at the tools on the floor. Useless, with the undead security guards pinning his arms.

"You may let him go now," Ulricke addressed the two. "Our Mr. Morrison isn't going anywhere."

The burly men released their grip and once again moved behind their fearsome boss. Morrison, cold sweat beading his brow, turned to Deakin, the man who had led him into this trap.

"When did it happen, Charles? And how?"

"Earlier this afternoon. Like you, I was called into Ms. Klackenbach's office for a discussion. How could I refuse?" He threw a painful glance at her. She smiled and he nodded his head obediently.

"I think it went quite well," she said.

"And you think you can do the same to me?"

"Of course." Ms. Klackenbach and her throng of acolytes slowly advanced on Morrison.

"It happens to everyone who works here, sooner or later," said Fosworth, from the research department. His voice was dry and flat, as if he was talking about some company pension scheme.

"I won't tell anyone! I'll do my job quietly and never give you any trouble… Please. I don't want to be one of the undead!"

"It isn't as bad as all that, Dave," said Deakin. "In fact you'll even start to enjoy it. I know I certainly have. The freedom. The power. The sensations."

"Yes," someone else chimed in, from the back. "Being a vampire isn't at all as bad as it's painted."

"And it's not like being human is anything to write home about," insisted Mrs. Fulcrum. "Just read any newspaper."

"Please… I just want to stay the way I am. As a human being. Not a ghoul..."

"We all felt that way, at first," whispered Deakin. "But things are different now. And you'll find that out as well, Dave."

"I am offering you immortality, Mr. Morrison," purred Ms. Klackenbach. "No sickness. No death. No fear. You'll become the master of your own fate. Tell me… What other company offers benefits like that?"

"I don't want it. Any of it!"

"I'm sorry. Did you really believe you have a choice in the matter? Only our kind of people work in this office now." She smiled through glinting teeth. "We are just one, big, happy family."

Morrison took a few tentative steps back from the advancing multitude and found himself pressed against a wall. His legs suddenly felt like rubber, and he was inexplicably weak and exhausted.

No! his mind screamed. *There must be a way out. There must be!*

Ulricke Klackenbach removed her tinted glasses and carefully placed them on a ledge. Morrison saw for the first time the true shape and color of her cat-like eyes. She solemnly raised her arms and long black fringes hung from the sleeves of her gown, like the plumage of some exotic bird of prey. She fixed him with her ice-cold gaze, and Morrison felt the last of his will and resistance drain away.

"There's no point in resisting, David," she purred in a soft, velvety voice that somehow echoed violently within his skull. "It is time to accept the inevitable. As all the others have done."

He felt her cold, stale breath on his neck. He shuddered and stiffened as two sharp pointed teeth penetrated the soft flesh of his neck, as gobs of his life's blood drained into her thirsty mouth.

"Just go with the flow…," she murmured, as all his pain and terror ebbed like the tide, and he slipped deeply into darkness.

He fought back up through a fog of consciousness to find himself still pressed against the wall. He couldn't be sure how long he was under, but when his eyes reopened, Ulricke and the others were in virtually the same position, staring at him.

All those monsters...

His coworkers… His friends…

His people…

And suddenly, the darkness melted away, replaced by a delicious, dreamy euphoria, beyond anything he had ever experienced.

"There now," said Deakin, with a sympathetic smile. "That wasn't too bad, was it?"

All the knotted tension, fear and strain of the day dissolved into an ineffable contentment such as he had never felt before. It hadn't been a bad day after all.

On his drive home, navigating the traffic had often been a source of frustration. Yet tonight, David Morrison felt light and blissful, entirely at peace with the world.

It wasn't bad at all, you know, he mused to himself. *Not bad at all.*

Once inside his home, he retrieved a pack of cigarettes hidden in the front pocket of a little-used jacket that hung from a rack. *Who needs these now?* he wondered, then tossed the pack into a wastepaper bin.

"So you've seen the light at last," exclaimed Janet with a smile.

"And this time there's no going back," he smiled at his wife. How beautiful she looked in the pale evening light.

How deliciously beautiful…

She squinted curiously at his blissful expression. "Well, you certainly seem more cheerful now," she said.

"To tell the truth, I've never felt better."

"So it wasn't as stressful a day as you thought it would be?"

"Well, that's imagination for you. It paints pictures in the mind that rarely match reality. It seems I got all worked up over nothing. It was a pleasant surprise actually. It was all clear sailing. Nothing to get stressed up about at all." He moved closer to his wife.

"Yes, I think I'm really fitting in at work now," he smiled. "Becoming a part of the team."

"Well, that's good to hear." She looked up at him with concern. "Though you do look rather pale, David. I hope you're not coming down with something. Perhaps you should see a doctor?"

"I don't think so. It's been a good day, but I do feel rather… drained. But nothing a good night's sleep won't cure. Why don't you and I call it a night?" he asked, as he took her small warm hand in his cold one.

And by morning, it wasn't just her husband's face that the mirrors of the house were no longer able to reflect.

Ancestors not Calm

Vin Morreale, Jr.

If, as author Alyson Richman claims, "*...we are always connected to our ancestors; our bodies hold the memories of those who came before us, whether it is the features we inherit or a disposition that is etched into our soul...*" then many of us must have had a frenetic background indeed.

A deeper understanding of who we are may be gained by looking back before we were born, tracing that seemingly random string of genetic, experiential and behavioral mutations which contribute to the individuality of us all. As such we become not only the product of our own experiences, fears and nightmares, but those of our parents and our parents' parents as well. Though we may find that many of our family trees are more gnarled and twisted than we would like to believe.

If we go back far enough, much of humanity can trace their ancestors to various tribes of Stone Age people, whose primary goal in life was simply to eat whatever they could pick, catch or bludgeon, while trying not to be caught, eaten or bludgeoned by the various forces of unfathomable nature around them.

A case in point is an early prehistoric specimen known to his clan as Horunth, who earned a barely-vocalized reputation as a fierce fighter and brave hunter. Horunth wore a proud pelt from an aging, half-blind saber-tooth tiger. Yet, as always reputations are often more exaggerated than earned.

As the unfortunate beast pawed its way across a tangled mat of branches, the shifting wood creaked and groaned underneath the tiger's six hundred pound weight. It was then that the formidable creature recognized a particular scent, a slight odor of fresh meat wafted teasingly over the boulders and cervices. Despite its feeble eyesight and aging muscles, a predatory instinct overwhelmed the senses of the savage beast and a guttural roar welled up from its nearly empty belly, as saliva dripped burst forth from its savage jaws.

Horunth, aging and overweight himself, had chosen that particular point in time to forage for berries in the nearby woodland. The moment he heard the fearsome roar, his natural instincts took over.

He evacuated his bladder in fear.

His next instinct was to try to run, but despite his panic, or perhaps because of it, his moistened legs would not move.

On the ridge above, the aging feline tightened its haunches in the tensile crouch that would, in an instant, propel a ferocity of claws and teeth through the air, and onto its terrified, unresisting prey.

Dozens of centuries before organized religion, Horunth gurgled out an incomprehensible prayer to the equally incomprehensible *Anyone Who Could Hear* and *Anyone Who Would Help*, in the hope there was some small chance he could survive what he knew was a certain, and a mostly certainly painful death.

Perhaps it was the prayer, or simply the randomness of chaos, but Fate did indeed intervene on the part of the tiger's quaking, urine covered prey. As the saber-tooth intensified his crouch, the groaning branches decided they wanted no part of the slaughter to follow. A sapling under the beast's rear haunches cracked, split and escaped down a deep crevice. Before the amazed eyes of the frightened caveman, the tiger roared, sprang slightly into the air, then hovered for an instant without moving. Their widened eyes met, predator and prey, and the stunned look on the animal's face matched the stupefied expression of its intended victim. With a whimpering mewl, the saber-tooth tiger disappeared down the crevice, vicious paws clawing desperately at air molecules too insubstantial to support its massive weight, as the great beast crashed onto the rocks eighty feet below.

For a brief eternity, time being a concept far beyond Horunth's comprehension, the little caveman stood motionless, expecting the tiger to suddenly reappear in a flurry of razor sharp pain above his head. After a few hours, the heavy sun roused the blinking primitive from his stupor, and the slow realization that he had survived certain death made him shiver twice as much as before.

He *had* survived, but how? The cause and effect relationship of heavy animal and thin branches was as lost on the caveman's feeble mind as it had been to the tiger. To Horunth, there could only be one explanation. The all-knowing *Anyone Who Could Hear* or the incomprehensible *Anyone Who Would Help* had somehow grabbed the massive beast in mid-pounce, held it in mid-air, then tossed the monster casually down onto the sharpened rocks.

Horunth tripped slowly over to the edge of the cliff and stared down at the motionless form of the great beast. Although its back was twisted in an impossible position, its lifeless arms still appeared to be clawing at the insubstantial sky. Horunth growled at it, softly at first, them with increasing confidence once the beast did not acknowledge his challenge. Horunth grunted, then yelled, then laughed and danced his defiance at the edge of the eighty-foot cliff. Still, the creature did not respond. Only then did enlightenment creep upon the little man's primitive mind. Horunth had survived!

Horunth was protected! Horunth was special! Horunth was a force to be reckoned with!

To seal his triumph, Horunth urinated on the great beast from his safe vantage point, many yards above. It was a fitting revenge. Then he kicked over a few stones which cascaded down the rocky summit, picked up some companions, and landed with multiple thuds to pummel the monster's powerful limbs. Still the beast did not rouse. Only when the curious sun lost interest and began to drift westward, did the caveman begin to make his way down the mountainside to his predator turned prey.

It was near dusk when Horunth reached the body of the sabertooth. He approached it cautiously, still unsure whether it would suddenly rouse to life in some cruel bit of animal humor. He circled it repeatedly, but it still refused to move. A large puddle of blood leaking from its head had begun to attract insects; the massive hunter being itself slowly devoured by minuscule predators. The air was beginning to chill as the sun slumped below the horizon. And with the advent of darkness, Horunth was unsure of what to do. Surely, this was the biggest prize any hunter in his clan had ever aspired to. Horunth's clan was not known to be mammoth hunters, or to chase anything more terrifying that a lost baby boar. And here, he had conquered a great, fearsome beast; for in his own mind, he began retelling the battle with a far more active role.

The distant howls of hunters in the darkness reminded Horunth that his proximity to the massive carcass might bring other jaws to bear on his throat. It was far too late to find his way back to cave and clan. A man alone in the night was just as likely to fall off a cliff, as fall prey to nighttime predators. In fact, any clan member that did not return to his cave by nightfall was presumed to never return at all. As savage roars and growls filled the evening air, Horunth's salvation seemed hollow indeed. Would the incomprehensible *Anyone Who Would Help* save his life, only to watch night marauders feast on his bones? Why couldn't the *Anyone Who Would Help* pick Horunth up as easily as it had plucked the much heavier tiger out of the air and deliver him to the safety of his cave? Had Horunth somehow offended the fickle *Anyone Who Could Hear?*

As night fell in curtains of black despair, Horunth noticed more and more pairs of cold green eyes peering from the outskirts of his vision. They hung on the edge of shadows, filled with chilling hatred and burning hunger. The scent of a tiger may keep them at bay a little longer, but eventually its own death smell would call to them like a dinner bell from miles around.

Horunth wept for the cruelty of this world.

Yet, an innate sense of survival often overcomes the equally primal need for self-pity. Horunth roused himself from his tears and began gathering twigs and grasses for a fire. He struck his flint chip against a sharp rock and blew on the sparks until the grasses began to smolder.

His next step was to pick up handfuls of dirt and bury the puddle of blood oozing out of the tiger's skull. The smell of blood might be too powerful a magnet to overcome even a night creature's fear of fire. Horunth had to cover half the tiger's massive head in dirt. Then he laid himself underneath the tiger's heavy paws and snuggled his rump against its massive belly, which by all rights and logic, he should have been snuggling from inside the stomach of the great cat. Yet, there he lay, hugged like a lover by the still warm carcass of the savage beast, until he fell asleep out of terror and boredom.

Perhaps it was the scent of the great beast which permeated his dreams. Or maybe it was the voice of *Anyone Who Could Hear.* Whatever the inspiration, Horunth's dreams were filled with images of enormous fanged creatures stalking him; saber-toothed tigers the size of wooly mammoths, cunning wolf packs, and man-sized vultures with skin-tearing beaks. And so he ran, ran as fast as he could, but his hungered tormentors were always at his heels, closing in for the kill. He found himself at the edge of the precipice, staring down over the cliff. There, on the rocks below, lay the great saber-toothed tiger. Suddenly, it leapt straight up into the air, landing easily on the rocks at his feet. He was trapped, a dozen ravenous monsters behind him, the great beast before him. The pack of predators closed in. The tiger crouched, ready to strike. Although he would not realize it until he awoke, the caveman again leaked liquid fear down his leg.

With a teeth-rattling roar, the tiger pounced. Horunth screamed, but did not feel the tearing claws, the crushing weight or the hot, snarling breath. Instead, the tiger flew completely over him and attacked the dozen hungry predators. In a whirlwind of destruction, its massive jaws filled with bloodied fur from the throats of howling wolves and screaming vultures. The bestial battle kicked up clouds of dust that nearly obscured the fearsome scene, as each predator fell before the great cat. In the end, only the saber-tooth stood, proud, vicious, and unscathed. It raised its massive head in a cavern-splitting roar that drove Horunth to his knees in terror. Then the great beast turned to the little caveman and bowed its head. Horunth looked at the torn and bloody carcasses of the wolf pack and finally understood the image. Surely, this great cat was his totem. A powerful protector embodying both *Anyone Who Could Hear* and *Anyone Who Would Help.* Its subservient bow made Horunth realize that he no longer need fear the outside world. He was man! He was powerful! The jaws of beasts would never again have dominion over him!

Horunth awoke to a stiff member and a feeling of power he had never felt before. He was still cradled in the heavy forearms of the great cat but felt no fear under its crushing weight. The fire had long since subsided into angry red embers, yet no animal had dared approach his campsite. It was as it should be. Horunth the mighty, Horunth the Tiger Slayer. No beast dared confront him again.

Horunth rose and growled his defiance to the world.

It took most of the morning to skin the massive tiger. He sliced open its thick belly with his flint knife, and gently peeled the fur away from sinew, meat and skeleton. It was a job that required great care, or this magnificent pelt would be ruined. He smiled as he imagined the looks of disbelief that his mate would wear as he re-emerged from the clearing wearing a tiger-skin wrap. Surely they would see he was One Who Knew No Fear, for that is what he had named himself after his night of omens.

Horunth decided to leave the huge skull in place, as part of the fur. He sliced off some muscle above the huge forearm and ate it slowly. What would he do with the rest of the beast? Surely this was too great a prize to leave for scavengers. Then Horunth noticed a large green profusion at the base of the cliff. A banana fern offered its wide green leaves to the newly anointed One Who Knew No Fear. This gave Horunth an idea, an occurrence that had not happened very often in his life. He wrapped the tiger's carcass in greta leaves, used his flint knife to slice off meat for the long journey back, then buried the massive carcass under a large pile of stones. He pulled the fur pelt around his shoulder, surprised by its still considerable weight, then began the long, painful trudge out of the ravine.

He stopped only to squeeze precious water from the small ram's bladder he kept tied to his waist, the makeshift canteen had been scraped clean and tied with a vine cord -- a trophy of the only other animal he had hunted alone.

Although he did not know why, predators avoided him the entire journey back to his cave. He attributed this blessing to his new divine protection from both *Anyone Who Could Hear* and *Anyone Who Would Help*, and it underscored the confidence in his own invulnerability. More likely, the scent of the fearsome beast, still fresh on its pelt, kept wary predators at bay, despite the fact that the distinctive fur markings were now trudging along on two hairy, but furless legs. Horunth was weary to the bone under the weight of his rare prize, but knew instinctively he must continue, or he would probably die out here in the open, unprotected spaces. Surviving two nights out in the open would be more than he could ever expect from his divine benefactors. He longed for the dark comfort of his cave, with its cold but comforting stone walls. He longed for the familiar scowls of those who shared his fire. The pale yellow fireball again hung low in the sky when Horunth finally reached the perimeter of his clan's dwellings.

He smiled as he approached his small group of primitive companions. There was Urghtha, and the tangle-haired female with large protrusions on her chest, squatting by her fire. He considered this too, a blessing from above.

No member of the clan had ever survived a night in the open before. Surely, they would be glad to see him. Instead, they scattered. The yelps, hisses and grunts of his companions reflected fear and confusion, more than recognition. The sight of Horunth's legs protruding from a saber-toothed tiger's pelt, stumbling unsteadily towards them, was twice as frightening as the beast itself. Twelve pair of caveman legs propelled a dozen terrified Cro-Magnons in a dozen different directions, leaving Horunth, the hunter, suddenly alone in his own village. He was alone again and could scarcely bear it. He fell to the ground in despair and wailed to the sky in a loud, pitiful moan.

Even though he shook the pelt from his shoulders, it took more than an hour before his companions emerged from their hiding places. They approached hesitantly at first. Ullggh, the mighty hunter. Arrgha, the child, and his sire with no name. Then the crippled hag-woman, followed by the tangle-haired Urghtha with the large chest protrusions. Each crept towards him tentatively, drawn by his wails of despair and a curiosity they could not shake. Here was a lost clan member returned from the dead! Beside him lay the skull and skin of their most deadly enemy. No one in their clan had ever killed a saber-tooth before. It was too strong, too fast, too ferocious. It would be like pulling the yellow fireball from the sky, too much for their primitive minds to conceive. Yet that potent smell was undeniably Horunth the Lost, of whom tales had already been sung around the fire. The unmistakable wail also spoke of Horunth the Lost, whom cave paintings had already immortalized. When he began beating the dirt with his clawed hands, they grew bold enough to poke him with sticks, then bony fingers. He snarled back at them as no vapor could. His growls of frustration drove them back a few feet. But when he pissed on their fire in haughty contempt, they knew Horunth the Lost was suddenly Horunth the Returned, and new tales must now be told, more vivid cave paintings must be drawn. And Horunth the Returned was suddenly embraced as the clan's greatest hero.

For five days and nights, the clan celebrated the return of one of their own from the terrifying ravages of the outside world. In their guttural language of clicks, grunts and gestures, Horunth related his adventure time and again. Each rendition was told with larger gestures, more fearsome snarls and greater bravery. The youngest of the clan, the last to tire of the story, were finally led to believe that Horunth had walked up to an entire pride of saber-tooths, snatched the largest by the throat, then pulled off its head and pelt, while the rest of the creature's body scampered away in fear.

A few suns later, Horunth led the strongest clan members on a trip to dig up the remains of the tiger. The decaying meat would feed the clan for an entire month. None had ever tasted sweet tiger meat, and Horunth became an even bigger hero with each meal. As a sign of his newfound status, the tangle-haired female with large protrusions on her chest shared his cave corner for the first time.

The saber-tooth skull was mounted at the entrance to his cave, and the remainder of the pelt was fashioned into an outer garment that would forever trumpet his achievements. Compared to the goatskin pelts of his companions, Horunth looked positively regal, and his growing arrogance raised his lip in a proud, continuous snarl. Although Urrgh clearly had more skill as a hunter, Horunth was chosen to lead the males on hunting expeditions, where he supervised the killing of smaller and slower animals.

Horunth had never been happier.

After a full season of such treatment, Horunth the Returned, hero of the clan, favored by *Anyone Who Could Hear* and *Anyone Who Would Help*, committed the same fatal error that would plague mankind for eons to come.

He began to take his own reputation seriously.

As the warm season drew to a close, Horunth had become fattened as much by his status as first-among-eaters, as by his own legend. Even in those primitive days, our ancestors displayed the all-too-human weakness of eventually believing the lies we tell about ourselves. Although he often awakened in night terror, jostling the sleeping form of the tangle-haired woman, Horunth came to accept as truth his own exaggerated tale of adventure. He came to believe he had indeed waded into a den of saber-tooths and slaughtered a few dozen with his bare hands and savage teeth. He soon began to believe he was even stronger than either *Anyone Who Could Hear* or *Anyone Who Would Help*.

No matter how bright the sun, constant exposure inevitably becomes tiresome and irritating. After two seasons, and a substantial girth added to his mid-section, the tale of Horunth the Returned began to lose its excitement. Soon, even the youngest clan-dwellers would not listen to the tale, preferring instead to scamper off to play Horunth and The Tiger whenever the real Horunth approached. Even the tangle-haired woman with the large chest protrusions grew bored at sharing a fire with the overweight legend.

Horunth had made the final transition in status. He unwittingly assumed the role of revered annoyance.

As he squatted alone by his now-meager fire, grunting his tired tale of bravery to the lonely walls, he had never felt more wretched or unwanted. In the sorrowful shadows of his cave, Horunth suddenly grasped the second big idea of his life. A tiger pelt had won him honor in the past. A second tiger pelt would win him even greater acclaim!

The next darkness, Horunth gathered the clan around his fire to announce the great mission. Although not everyone understood his grunts, clicks and sweeping fist movements, they knew Horunth the Returned was leaving to do something amazing. The tangle-haired woman rubbed his greasy thigh with renewed delight.

On a cold, overcast morning, Horunth, clad in his now-tattered tiger pelt, stomped proudly from the clan dwelling to find and conquer another, even bigger saber-toothed tiger. He carried a sharpened stick, a primitive knife of rough-hewn flint, and the ever-present sneer that curled his lip. The clan growled and yelped encouragement as their hero, the greatest clan hunter who had ever lived, walked alone into the terrifying outworld.

Needless to say, Horunth the Returned never did... earning him even greater status in clan legends. His final thought as gnashing death sprang upon him was a stunned and desperate cry to the *Anyone Who Could Hear* and *Anyone Who Would Help* for so unjustly abandoning him.

It is likely that many unnamed descendants would also have vanished in that long ago shredding of worn pelt, flesh and ego, had it not been for the swelling belly of the tangle-haired woman with even larger protrusions on her chest.

For reasons known only to themselves, it seemed that *Anyone Who Could Hear* and *Anyone Who Would Help* had chosen to preserve Horunth's line, instead of the legend himself.

Such is the wisdom of divinities.

OUR AUTHORS

Most of the stories in this collection represent winning entries in the *Academy Arts 2019 Short Story Contest.*

First Prize: $150.00

Gills / Gary Wadley - Louisville, Kentucky

Second Prize: $100.00

The Biscuit Board /Mary Popham - Louisville, Kentucky

Additional Winners:

Great Friends / Marc Hockl – Cleves, Ohio

Doc / David Gaylor – Dayton, Ohio

The Rest Of The World / Gary Wadley - Louisville, Kentucky

Blithe / Margie Marek – Mahopac, New York

Beyond The Sea / Ross Touhy – Alvechurch, UK

Flight Of The Eye / Sheri Hawthorne Carbone - Louisville, Kentucky

The House With Two Front Doors / Lucy Mills – Kent, UK

Newspaper Man / Malarie Drake – Bowling Green, Kentucky

Ulricke Klackenbach / Michael Noonan –West Yorkshire, UK

Not in Competition:

Would I? Could I? Should I? / Mandy Morreale - Prospect, Kentucky

Strange Impressions / Victor Salia – San Francisco, California

Ancestors not Calm / Vin Morreale, Jr. - Prospect, Kentucky

To find more creative works of fiction and fun, or to enter this year's *Academy Arts Press Short Story Competition*, please visit academyartspress.com.

ALSO FROM ACADEMY ARTS PRESS

ACADEMYARTSPRESS.COM.

Short Fiction Collections

Knowing When To Leave / Vin Morreale, Jr.

Dark Wilderness & Other Stories / Vin Morreale, Jr.

Humor

Chicken Fat for the Damaged Psyche / Vin Morreale, Jr.

The Best of Senseless Bickering / Vin Morreale, Jr.

Acting Resource Books

Two Character Chaos / Vin Morreale, Jr.

300 Monologues / Vin Morreale, Jr.

150 Acting Scenes / Vin Morreale, Jr.

Illustrated Children's Books

Mabel The Maple / Vin Morreale, Jr. & Jessica Lee

Too Many Rules / Vin Morreale, Jr. & Mandy Morreale

My Brother Has Autism / Mandy Morreale

T1D & Me / Mandy Morreale

Stage Plays

The Kiss Me Curse / Vin Morreale, Jr.

All My Passions / Vin Morreale, Jr. ***(Summer 2020)***

The Carrie Variations / Vin Morreale, Jr. ***(Fall 2020)***

www.ingramcontent.com/pod-product-compliance
Lightning Source LLC
Chambersburg PA
CBHW071527100726
47908CB00004B/1312

* 9 7 8 1 7 3 4 7 3 1 3 1 6 *